AFTERLIFE

EXPERIENCES MAY VARY

JET GARNER

ATLANTA

Dedicated to my oldest niece, Abigail Stanton.
Without realizing it, I had you in mind while creating this novella to be accessible for younger readers.
I hope this short book fits within your voracious reading appetite.

Author's Note

This story has a special significance in my career as a writer. After umpteen years, it was the first thing I'd written in a very long time. It sparked my desire to write the stories developing in my imagination.

Similar to *Death in the Afternoon*, my debut novel, this idea began in Moab, Utah. I wrote it as a short story for a contest, where it performed well. It won me fifty bucks!

Most writers don't get a dime for their first story. I felt both fortunate and privileged a 5,000 word short earned me anything.

Back then, it was titled *Mr. Bones*. After beginning the journey of bringing *Mr. Bones* to life in a deeper work, I decided it needed a different title—because, as all works do when you rewrite them—the story changed significantly.

The writing began in Puerto Peñasco, Mexico, where my wife and I stayed for three weeks. We were recovering from an eighteen day rafting trip, two hundred and fifty miles through the Grand Canyon with family and friends. Soon after that trip, we found ourselves in Kuala Lumpur, Malaysia, which is where the majority of this novel was created. I'm proud to say it concluded in Ho Chi Minh (Saigon), Vietnam, and we finished the editing just after buying a condo in Chiang Mai, Thailand.

It's been an eventful year, to say the least.

As I write to you, it is pouring down rain in northern Thailand on September 24th, 2024. I'm sitting at a restaurant called The Writer's Club founded by an English journalist and his wife since there wasn't a writer's hangout when he moved to Chiang Mai. It felt fitting to write this letter to my readers while sitting at the establishment where we finished editing the book you're holding—*Afterlife*.

I sit here six months from when we published *Death in the Afternoon* in March. And the second novel in the Psychopomp Anthology should be ready early next year.

Busy, busy.

Such is the life of a nomadic author, I suppose. If any of you ever consider it yourself, I highly recommend marrying your editor. I can't imagine how this process would look and feel if Crystal wasn't part of the journey every step of the way.

Although this book isn't dedicated to her (the last one was), I feel her spirit is found just as often among these pages as the previously published ones. That is something I personally love about my work. I love that it is *our* work as much as it is mine. It makes the satisfaction deeper when someone enjoys reading something that I've written. It also builds my pride in the product, because it is something tangible—real—that we've created together.

Enough about me. Let's talk about the work.

For starters, this is a satirical book. I think it's important to get that declaration out of the way.

My first novel was far more serious. Humor was present, but it was frequently washed away with blood. This book is radically different.

When I conceived this idea, it was 2021. COVID had just finished having its way with the world via politics and health organization restrictions. Like most people, this frustrated me. I wanted to lash out. So, I lashed out.

I created a man named Reverend Raymond Carter, and I took my frustration out on him.

Religion has always been a complicated subject for me. Without going down a ferret hole about it, I am profoundly skeptical of it as a whole. I am critical of religion and its impact on humanity. And I'm good at history. There are many aspects of the past I will likewise never forgive regarding religion.

On a lighter note, I just wanted to mention that for anyone that reads this, I'm not attempting to directly insult anyone with the words in this book. Instead, my aim is to entertain you with a satirical circumstance that has elements of comedy, consequences, and conflict with the unknown.

Is it meant to challenge whatever your beliefs are? Not really, no. Are the words supposed to be thought provoking? Definitely. What I want to point out is I am telling you a story that is meant to be entertaining as well as make you think. All I ask is to read this work of satire with an open mind.

With that out of the way, I hope the pages you turn make you smile. I hope some of them make you laugh. I may even get a tear or two out of you occasionally. It wouldn't surprise me if sometimes you become uncomfortable or angry. All of those feelings are acceptable responses to the novel in your hands.

The essence of this book is about life, spirit, and how ridiculous things can be in our lives. I suppose with this letter to you out of the way, I'll let you get to it.

Say hello to Raymond Carter for me when you see him. How similar life is to turning the pages of a book. As I close this book and set it down, you are picking it up for the first time.

Enjoy the ride.

— Jet Garner

Part I

Reverend Raymond Carter

Chapter One

Reverend Raymond Carter was spending his last days preparing to meet God. One may think that statement is obvious. What else would someone in his position be doing besides such a thing? However, whoever makes this supposition must not know Raymond Carter.

Raymond Carter is the pastor of an enormous nondenominational church in Houston, Texas. His local congregation numbers between forty thousand and fifty thousand souls. Nationally, his flock is innumerable. Despite the gargantuan size of Meadowview Megachurch, the stadium seating can accommodate a staggering fifty-five thousand people. Although he has never filled the seats during a single sermon, he fills most of them every Sunday.

On his deathbed at Houston Methodist Hospital, Reverend Raymond lies alone in his quarantined room. The incessant beeping of his vital signs on monitors infuriated him. But most of all, he loathed the hoses running in and out of his body. Hoses ran into his nostrils, providing him with pure oxygen. Tubes connected to I.V. drips made their way into catheters in both of his hands. Much to his dismay, he even had a hose plugged into his urethra, because he lacked the capability to make it to the restroom to relieve himself. Raymond Carter is dying of Covid-19.

When the Federal Government recommended the nation remain indoors and at home to prevent the transmission of the deadly virus,

Raymond had insisted his church stay open. Many arguments were made against this decision. His successful televangelist broadcast made people ask why require physical attendance at the church? Why risk personal and congregational health when it is easy to avoid by staying home? His members could choose to stay home, but he was too young to be killed by Covid-19. If God's plan was to remove him from his physical form on Earth, so be it. In God's clean spirit, he would not close his doors because of mankind's interventions.

He, of course, caught Covid and was hospitalized within a week of beginning to cough. That was only two weeks ago. Now, doom was inevitable. Raymond could feel his body losing this battle against his unseen foe. Accepting his fate with the confidence of his faith in the Lord was one of the proudest moments of Raymond's life. Praise God.

Besides knowing that he would soon meet his creator, the only reprieve from Raymond's plight was his mobile phone. This provided him with his guilty pleasure. A happiness that does not sprout from his devotion to God. Nor does it come from his vast fortune or undisputed success as a pastor. It likewise cannot be diminished by the bleakness of his hospital cell. Raymond didn't let the many hoses, machines, the repeated monotony of reruns of his sermons on his TV, or even death keep him down. He maintained a rich fantasy life to occupy his fully functional mind. Thankfully, the reverend's nearly nonstop prayers to meet God were broken up by a persistent stream of concerned girls via social media.

Being a forty-three-year-old man did not stop Reverend Raymond Carter from thoroughly enjoying the attention, affection, and pursuit of young women. The gifts of influence, faith, and financial freedom provided him with all the female attention he could stand. And he could stand a great deal of it, praise God.

He spent many hours of his time in the hospital documenting and posting on his various social media accounts. He posted videos daily about what he was going through and how it affected his life. Raymond wanted to be remembered for his bravery while facing his demise. How devout and trusting in his own message he truly was. This was to be the magnus opus of his social standing. The ultimate sacrifice that elevated him to Heaven. Reverend Raymond Carter also desired his ordeal to gain the affection of as many women as possible.

Some of these women were mature in age. Thirty-something's or forty-something's, for example. Raymond didn't pay them much mind, though. They weren't the type of girls he wanted affections from. He would only talk to women of that age if it served a specific purpose through his ministry or his medical treatment. A purpose beyond simple desire. The girls Raymond Carter wanted conversations with weren't necessarily children, but many people wouldn't consider them full-fledged women, either.

He relished conversations and meetings with females in the late teens or twenties. It made him feel desirable. The relationships didn't have to get physical to get his blood pumping. Raymond adored to be adored, and online or social media attention was all he needed from his younger fans. The occasional skimpy photo never hurt, of course. Nothing serious. Raymond was careful about anything that could negatively impact his social standing. Social status, above all else (except for his position with God) is what mattered to Reverend Carter. After all, cleanliness is next to godliness. And that was sort of how he saw social standing. To have good standing was to be without tarnish. Tarnish sounded dirty.

God and he had an understanding about his vices. Of this, he was certain. It was society that couldn't understand him. Society which would judge him. Raymond knew only one power could judge him when he stood before Heaven and awaited Saint Peter to allow him to enter through the alabaster gates. And that power was not society. In a way, Raymond looked over society the way God looked over him. His flock looked up to him and he looked up to God. It was to be God that would judge Reverend Raymond Carter.

As his condition declined and breathing became more and more difficult, he struggled to curb his fear. It was becoming increasingly hard for him to relay his videos and messages while keeping the fear hidden. Raymond was succeeding, but it required effort. He hadn't been prepared to actually contract the virus. Much less be hospitalized by it. Laying in his crinkly, plastic covered hospital bed alone, Raymond juggled his time between praying to the Lord and preying on his phone. Unfortunately, all the co-ed affections in the world couldn't stave off Covid-19's axe.

Amidst one of his many prayers, Raymond once again called on God for a miracle, and wipe the coronavirus from his body. Asked Him to cleanse the taint of the wasting virus from his lungs. Putting all the girls and fantasies out of his mind, Raymond poured his entire focus into this most desperate of prayers. Almost as if in response, he took a long, deep breath that didn't hurt. It was the first breath that didn't hurt in more than a week. Holding that wonderful air in his lungs as long as he could stand it, he let it out, looking forward to the next one. It didn't come.

Reverend Raymond Carter never breathed again.

Chapter Two

Raymond laid there unmoving as the room began swarming with people. Two nurses dressed like a hazmat team raced in at the alarm that sounded a few moments after he failed to take his second breath. A doctor and yet more nurses followed those two. Everyone of them was wearing ridiculous poofy yellow scrubs that covered every inch of their bodies and plastic face shields over their already masked mouths. They had opened his gown and attached a defibrillator to his chest. The room burst into chaos as they shouted different commands to each other in practiced symphony. What startled Raymond the most is that he remained conscious throughout all of this.

He was aware of all that happened around him. Heard the alarm when he... stopped breathing? Stopped breathing. Then the medical team had rushed in and put those sticky nodes on his chest. Why weren't they cold? It was dreadfully drafty in his room. Raymond would catch a chill whenever he wasn't covered by the sheet and blanket the hospital had provided him. Surely those electric pads on the defibrillator would be chilly, wouldn't they?

The doctor pushed a button on the wall, and the alarm ceased its howling. The oscilloscope that displayed his vitals wailed a single tone instead of the blipping he had heard earlier. A nurse reached over and silenced it. They all looked down at him for a moment. They exchanged a few words, then most of them left. Two remained, and they began removing the system of tubing from his body that Raymond had hated so much.

What was happening? He remembered how itchy and uncomfortable some of the tubes were. The adhesive itched on the backs of his hands where the I.V. catheters plunged into the blue-green veins through his skin. He couldn't feel anything anymore. The pesky hose that ran into his genitals had *always* been uncomfortable. It *always* scratched and created pressure in the space it occupied. There was never a reprieve from *that* shameful plumbing intervention. Yet now, as they slid it out of him, not only did he not feel relief, but he indeed felt nothing. How was that possible?

With the hoses removed and the electronics measuring his vitals silenced, the remaining nurses tucked him into his covers and left the room. Raymond tried calling out to them, but nothing happened. His eyes stared unblinking at the ceiling; his head and neck impossibly stiff and unresponsive. Raymond waited and waited. When were the nurses coming back? Had he...?

Going over the reality of events in his mind, Raymond decided he must have died. It was the only logical explanation. The unsettling result of this deduction is that if he had died, why was he still here? Why was he laying unmoving in his hospital bed? He tried moving again. Nothing.

Panic stirred within Reverend Carter as he tried to move his head to look at the door. He tried to call out for help. A second opinion. Anything. He remained still as a coffin. *What was the meaning of this?* He thought with incredulity. *What in the hell is going on?*

After swearing in his mind, Raymond immediately asked God for forgiveness. Maybe this was normal. Maybe it took time for one's soul to leave their body after death. That must be it. Raymond forced himself to relax. He wished he could take a deep breath. Alas, he couldn't.

The reverend decided to let whatever this process was to run its course. Besides, the situation didn't seem to allow him any choice, anyway. He had lived forty-three years on this planet as God's messenger and disciple. If anyone possessed the discipline to trust in God and get through this with dignity, it was he. It must take a good bit of time for a soul to ascend after the earthly body dies. This was probably normal. After all, it isn't written anywhere what the passage of energy really looks like after death occurs.

Steeling himself against the rising fear threatening his resolve, Raymond waited. Since he couldn't close his eyes, he imagined blackness in his mind. Blackness that would embrace his ebbing mind as his soul would slowly be released from its fleshy prison and ascend into Heaven the way scripture told him it would. Ascend into peace and tranquility and warm streets paved with gold. Rise into eternal light and love to be with the Lord.

Chapter Three

Raymond's meditational void shattered when a group of three nurses returned to his quarters. After tapping a few buttons and stomping a couple of devices on the bottom of the bed, Raymond was rolling. He tried to communicate in vain, but his body remained unresponsive.

Fluorescent lights and ceiling tiles passed by in consistent patterns. A nurse escorting the caravan pushed a panel on the wall to part doors for the other two, and further down the corridors he went. A turn here, an elevator there. Where were they taking him?

Hey, you two! C'mon, listen to me!

Raymond had never believed in telekinesis or ESP, but it didn't hurt to try. Mediums claimed to hear the voices of the dead. But, *after* you're dead, how does one hire the services of a medium?

You've got to hear me! Listen to me!

In his mind's ears, Raymond was shouting at them. Waving metaphorical arms at them. Trying desperately to get their attention. They continued their petulant gossip. A travesty was taking place right under their middle-aged noses (and middle-aged breasts, Raymond thought with distaste) and they were carrying on like tomorrow was senior prom.

"I don't know, Denise. I've never thought about Dr. Stewart like that. Do you *really* think they are swingers? How do you know?" a nurse, dressed more like a yellow and blue clad welder pushing his bed, said.

"Oh, I know for sure!" cooed the other medical welder on his left. "Tammy told me she went to one of those kinkster meetups last weekend and saw Stewart and his wife there."

"No," the other gal in scrubs gasped in disbelief. "They're meeting despite the stay home order from the CDC? Woah. How brave! Hm... well, I wonder what the um—criteria is to join their little swingers' club?" They both giggled.

"I'm not sure, but if that's true? As soon as all this world shutting down nonsense is over, sign me up!" She offered a playful gloved slap to the other's arm. "Stewart has always looked like a lot of fun. His wife is even kind of cute. I saw her without a mask a couple of times a few months back."

Raymond was fuming. He was supposed to be in Heaven! He should be negotiating with St. Peter and discussing the weight of his faith against his potential sins. He wasn't supposed to be consciously unconscious, getting wheeled around by a couple of wannabe-swinger nurses.

As their conversation lulled off, Raymond realized they had gotten into another elevator. Only the two pushing him continued on. The third nurse that was activating panels to open doors must not be needed where they were going. Watching the digital display above the doors, he saw they were going down. Passing the lobby, he noticed. They finally arrived at a lower level of the hospital.

Wheeling Raymond down another hallway, the nurses opened another set of double doors ahead of the bed. It led outside. They were taking him outside. Raymond was looking at a warm spring sky. It made him wish he could feel its warmth. It was odd seeing sunshine touch your skin and the sheets covering your body, but not feel it.

They arrived at a large parking lot with a dozen white trailers or more arranged in organized grids. The two women wheeled Raymond's gurney up a ramp to access an entrance to one pod. Upon opening the door, both nurses shivered.

"I hate going to these pop-up morgue boxes," one said, shrugging her shoulders up to her ears. "They should really hang coats or something for us out here!"

Morgue boxes!

'O-M-G Becka. You're *so* right!" the other replied. "We should suggest that at the next meeting! Coats outside the morgue boxes would make so much sense. I bet we could easily get that passed through the union. Think they'd give us a dollar raise *and* coats for the morgue?"

They wheeled the bed into the dimly lit trailer. Inside, cots set up similar to bunk beds lay squeezed together. Narrow aisles were all that separated the multiple rows of cots and sheet covered bodies. The beds towered above them like scaffolding. A body lay in every bed Raymond could see. He noticed the face shields the nurses wore were fogging up from their breathing and their scrubs shook from the cold. What in the hell kind of place was this?

"Ha!" Becka scoffed. "More than likely, we'll trade our dollar this year for coats! But hey," she said with a smirk as the rumbling gurney came to a stop. "We could probably convince Dr. Stewart to recommend it in our honor and *still* keep our dollar increase this year if we played our cards right."

Denise stomped on a brake lever connected to a wheel next to her foot. "Now *that* is a proper idea! Talk about win-win." The laughter died out as they rubbed their hands together for friction.

After surveying the pile, one of them spoke up.

"I can't believe how full these trailers have gotten," Denise said. "It's insane that all the beds got filled already."

"I know it. I just hate coming out here. Gives me the creeps. I've had nightmares about these morgue boxes several times. Let's dump off this poor soul and get back inside. I hate being in here."

As they gripped either side of him, Raymond got a glimpse of where he was to be left. His panic revitalized anew inside of his mind. The fear swallowing him like he had an anchor tied to his feet, and he was about to be thrown overboard into the depths.

There was no bed for him, but a pile of sheeted bodies at the back of the trailer between a row of the scaffolded beds. Some still had a sheet covering their pale, withered faces, but some didn't. It looked like the medical staff had originally tried to stack the bodies neatly, but that was long gone. Now, the dead lay stacked criss-cross to stabilize the growing mound.

"1, 2..." one of the nurses said. "3!" they shouted together, and heaved Raymond onto the stack atop another former life. Raymond was appalled. The only emotion that matched his disgust was his fear. How long was he to be left in this box? When was he ascending into Heaven?

Both nurses looked down at him. Thankfully, Raymond got positioned so that he could see them. His head was pushed up enough that he had a view of his surroundings, although the nurses were so close that they blocked most of it.

"So sad," Becka said as she leaned forward to cover his face with the sheet. "Should we cover his face, or leave it bare? Wasn't he kind of a big deal? A preacher or something, right?"

Denise looked at her with alarm. "You don't know who he was? He's the televangelist megachurch guy! That gazillionaire over at Meadowview, Reverend Raymond Carter. Only one of the wealthiest and successful single men in Houston. He was brave enough to keep his church open against the rules. I'm surprised God didn't spare him to tell ya the truth."

Becka shrugged. "Oh! Well, I have heard of him, of course. Published a bunch of religious books and on TV spreading the gospel and all that. I knew he was an important figure when he first checked into the hospital, but I didn't think he was *that* guy. Man, what a shame. I bet he never imagined he would end up like this."

The other looked down at him with pity again. "Yeah... it's a messed up time, Becka. A really messed up time. Leave the sheet off his face. Let him feel on top of the world before we have to stack someone else on top of him."

"Good idea," Becka said, and she laid the sheet down where it was across his shoulders.

The swell of pride that rose within Raymond at their conversation about him had distracted him from his panic for a moment. It was a welcome reprieve. He felt like he had already been dead longer than just a little while. Time passed so slowly, now that he couldn't move. Couldn't breathe. Couldn't look around naturally. A terrifying thought arced across his mind. *I wonder if they install lights in these ice boxes?*

As if in answer to his musings, the women turned and released the brakes on the hospital bed and began wheeling it towards the light of the exit. As they walked away from him, Raymond could see more and more of the trailer as they went.

The two rows of beds, more like cots or tight hammocks, stretched all the way back to the entrance. Both sides rose towards the ceiling in columns of dead bodies. He lay atop an X-shaped stack at the end because no beds seemed available for him to occupy. The reality of Raymond's situation was sinking into him. The nurses exited, and he saw the light disappearing as the door swung closed.

Please let there be light when it closes. Please don't cast me into complete darkness in this horrid place. Please, God, help me. I beg of you!

Raymond heard a *click* as the steel door shut, casting the morgue box into near darkness. Soft red lights came on as the door sealed. It reminded Raymond of a refrigerator light that worked in reverse. Thankful for the lights, Raymond sent a silent thank you to God.

Time passed as he lay there. How long or how short? Raymond had no idea. He began looking at the occupants in neighboring beds. He realized he could see the face of an elderly man near his feet, out of the periphery of his vision. A face frozen in death. He couldn't seem to take his mind off of it. Raymond's condition leaked terror into his racing thoughts.

He tried yelling. He tried moving again. His body had become a prison. Raymond began begging to God in his mind. Begging Him to free his soul. To ascend at last. What madness was this? What had he done? Was it the girls? Oh, God, could it have been the girls?

No. That was fear speaking. That was the devil's whispering. Raymond knew that the weight of his faith protected him from God's judgement. His repentance and dedication to the glory of God for his entire adult life was not in vain. This had to be part of the process. The process all noble souls go through as they either ascend or descend. There was no other possibility.

As Raymond Carter focused again on the red-lit face that stared blankly into the same void as his own, he began wondering if maybe pitch darkness would have been better than dim red lights.

Chapter Four

The wretched red lights blinked out as sunlight illuminated the pop-up morgue. Swinging open with a soft *creaking* sound, the door struck the side of the trailer. A bed was wheeled in by two nurses dressed in the hazmat clown suits that had become the new norm for hospital personnel.

Raymond's periphery focused on the old man's face at his feet, then refocused on the nurses and his new roommate. Would they dump this new guy on top of him? He prayed not. Relief washed over him as the gurney passed his aisle and turned down the following one.

So it has been at least a day since I died, he thought. *I wonder if it has been one day or two? What do you think?* It was a question asked to the elderly face. It became a silent shadow at his feet with the red lights out. As silent as Raymond's life lately. Painfully quiet. One would think that level of silence to be peaceful, but in the reverend's case, it added to the dismal feel of his isolated prison. Isolated, yet surrounded by roommates. Focusing on the face hidden by shadow, Raymond was ashamed to admit he had begun conversations in his head with the quiet fellow below him.

He heard the nurses plop the next resident onto the X-shaped pile of corpses at the end of the neighboring aisle. Without a word, they wheeled the bed towards the exit.

Hey. HEY! Raymond tried yelling again. *Please! I'm—I'm not quite dead yet! Or something...*

His body didn't listen to his commands yet again. As the nurses shut the door, the red lighting resumed. Without thinking about it, his focus went straight to the dead man's visage at his feet. With the shadows torn away, Raymond could see the demon-red pale mask looking at him.

Was it looking at him before? He swore it stared blankly ahead earlier. Had it... moved? *No. No, it didn't move. Just a trick of the light and my mind. My—dead mind?* Raymond wondered again why he remained in this odd position. Was this his soul, or his consciousness? Was there a difference?

God's teachings, of course, allude to a soul being immortal. The body dies, and the mind is part of the body. Raymond figured most people probably believe they remain themselves in the afterlife—in Heaven. Who else would they be? Did that stem from the soul, or from the conscious psyche? Raymond wasn't sure, and from the look of things, he'd never get the chance to further research the subject.

Raymond focused on the wrinkled red face again. *What are you seeing? Are you in there like me, or were you allowed to ascend to Heaven?* The unasked question fell hollow on the unchanged old man. His eyes betrayed no emotion whatsoever. He must have died peacefully based on the expression he wore. Raymond wondered what his face looked like in death. Did he have a noble visage after his passing, or did he have a ghoulish shriek of pain or fright?

He imagined the madness of these dozens of people in the trailer all being stuck inside their own minds, just as he was. Whether his soul was trapped or his mind was still active, whichever the case, were they like that too? Were they also screaming against the outrage of this reality? To die, but not ascend or descend—anywhere. Was he alone in this plight? Was this the path of the forsaken?

Had God forsaken him? The thought prompted him to pray, just in case God had kept Raymond's account open.

How long would he remain in this state of—whatever this was? How long would he remain in this morgue, for that matter? Were they even holding funerals this year with Covid ripping through politics these past few months?

How long must he lay here immobile with nothing but a red-lit mask of death at his feet to converse with?

Chapter Five

Sixty-three days had passed in the world of the living. For Reverend Raymond Carter, the time ticked by at an impossibly slow rate. Slowly, like watching the lower portion of glass in windows from mid-20th century farmhouses thicken over time. Whatever was left of his psyche felt like it was slipping away.

Raymond had developed a few activities in an attempt to hang on; to stave off the madness just a little longer. Whatever amount of time was needed to transition to Heaven at last. He maintained faith that he *would* ascend. This—this *circumstance* was going to end, eventually. It had to. Nothing could last forever. If this was a stage of the afterlife, then so be it.

In God's clean spirit, Raymond was prepared to wait it out. Praise God.

So what do you think, Theo? Do you think we're probably halfway there at this point?

Theo was the name given to Raymond's downstairs neighbor. Raymond begun calling him Theo 16 days into their journey together. Their journey into the afterlife. Their journey to Heaven, as Raymond began insisting on the 10th day or so. He insisted on this to himself, to Theo, and to all of their neighbors.

There's Pete, represented by a right foot sticking out from under a sheet two bunks above Raymond and at the end of his own feet. On the right side of the aisle, on the bunk across from Pete, laid Magda. Raymond noticed he could see Magda's eyes and hair 3 days after he met Theo. Her sheet thankfully didn't cover her face all the way. Above Magda was Jonas, represented by a left arm hanging down into Magda's space. Last but not least were Judah and Debra, who got laid on the neighboring aisle's X-shaped pile. Judah was laid there on day 2, Debra on day 18. Raymond wasn't entirely sure that Debra was female, because he couldn't see her face when she got wheeled in, but he was pretty sure he saw breasts tenting the sheet when she went by. So he called her Debra.

Nurses hadn't dropped anyone off in quite some time. Almost 45 days had passed since the hospital added any roommates for Raymond. There had been visitors, though, merely of a different type.

The visitors would come in and count the dead from time to time. Sometimes they would get closer and inspect under a sheet here or there. In fact, today, on the 63rd day, one of those odd sorts came and examined Raymond.

Raymond was engaged in a heated debate with Judah about interpretations of the gospel (Judah was an atheist and Raymond was attempting to save his soul, you see) and the visitor barged in, interrupting the debate, and walked over to Raymond.

It was a woman, an attractive one, and she wasn't wearing the typical clown suit worn by the nurses. The mystery woman had opened the door and done something the nurses never did. She closed it behind herself. It was the first woman he had seen outside of a hazmat suit and face shield in what seemed like ages.

Raymond was so shocked by the change of pace that he halted his debate with Judah. She was stunning. Her hair was up in a ponytail and she wore a simple jean jacket over a white tank-top that shone pink in the red light. If Raymond's eyes could move, they would have followed that bosom side-to-side and all around as she made her way down his aisle, inspecting bodies. She must have been in her late twenties. A little old for his preferred age, but young enough to catch his attention.

Her pattern was to stop at a column of bunks, remove the sheet from the top half of a body, skeptically look it over, and then cover it back up. Up and down the bunks, she checked with a calculating look on her face. Seeming not to find what she was looking for, she would move on to another column and continue her search.

What is she looking for, Theo? What could she—oh, shut it, Judah! I am done arguing with you for now! You insolent turd of an atheist! God forgive me, I shouldn't offend the already condemned. Theo, what do you think she could be looking for?

Raymond listened intently for anything betraying her purpose in his dwelling. He liked to imagine that not only was this trailer *his* more than it belonged to the other roommates, but that he was somehow also in charge of things. It was how it was when he was alive, so he figured it should remain the same in the afterlife. At least until he got to Heaven, then God could be back in charge. On Earth, Reverend Raymond was in charge, even in death.

Despite his listening, she didn't say a word. Just fluttering about over all the corpses, obviously searching in vain. When she made it to the end of the aisle, she looked at Raymond. Raymond thought if he had a pulse, it would have quickened. Her attention was giving him anxiety. It had been quite a while since he had received any attention from the female sex besides the not-so-loving care from the nurses before they tossed him on this heap of bodies like some ordinary plebeian. Clearly, if they were better at their jobs and caring for him, he wouldn't have died.

No matter, she was looking down at him. He was roughly eye level with her waist. She was blocking Theo, but looking at the delicate arch of her groin in those dark pants was worth not seeing Theo for a time. Praise God.

Abruptly, she bent over, studying his face. Her gloved hands gripped his shoulders, then moved to his sheet. Raymond was flabbergasted when she pulled the sheet down and revealed the majority of his body down to his knees.

What on earth is she doing, Theo? Is she—checking me out? Maybe she recognizes me! That must be it! She recognizes the late-great Reverend Raymond Carter! I bet she's a fan. Magda, you better not be watching this. This is a private show. This is just between me and miss perfect here. You butt out, Magda!

After a thorough analysis of him, the woman smirked. *If blood was still pumping through these veins...* Raymond thought. Hastily and with care, she covered Raymond back up again, exactly as she found him. She attempted the same fold of his sheet, revealing his collarbones and shoulders; the same angle it laid across his chest. Soon after, she turned and walked away. Raymond relished the look of her rump as she stalked back towards the entrance. The blinding fan of light created when she opened the door was ripped away when she slammed it behind herself.

Did you see that, Theo? I was what she was looking for. She examined Magda, Pete, and Jonas. Heck, she didn't even bother looking at you. She wanted me. Ha! The next aisle wasn't even worth visiting! Take THAT, Judah! You dead, doomed idiot! Forgive me, forgive me, Lord. But—ha!

A thought crossed his mind for a moment. *Could she have... no. Surely she couldn't have been some sort of messenger, could she? No... She was just another human, right, Theo?*

As he listened for Theo's retort, Pete interrupted.

Oh? You've had some experiences with otherworldly messengers, Pete? What kinds? Well, did she look like any of the kinds of messengers you've seen before?

Silence laid over the dead as thick as the cold.

Raymond gasped in his own way. *Really? How very interesting. So, you've seen angels that look just like humans before? Of course! The Lord has sent me a messenger! Finally! That's why she didn't even bother with any Covid precautions besides the gloves, which could be explained, I'm sure of it. Because she wasn't natural. By God, she must have been divine.*

Raymond felt relief wash over him as he tried to send warmth out to his new friends and associates. He had always felt so chosen in life. All the time. Chosen by God. Chosen by young women. Chosen to lead millions of souls to Jesus Christ during his life. They all trusted him. God had finally shown his hand at long last.

That woman would be his saviour. He wasn't sure why she hadn't freed him this visit, but maybe there were preparations to make, or maybe it wasn't the right time. That didn't matter. What mattered is he was noticed. Noticed, and he just knew that it was a good omen of things to come.

Glory be to God.

Chapter Six

The resident population of their long-term retirement home grew over the next 58 days. If business felt slow after Raymond arrived all those months ago, Covid sure was booming outside of his blood-red insulated walls. For 121 days, Raymond's body had remained in the same anatomical position. Despite all ideas for keeping track of time frozen atop Theo on their mound of bodies, none had proved fruitful. Reality was one long episode of the same timeless experience. The theological discussions and invented arguments had grown stale as Raymond watched the bodies stack in front of him.

His aisle had swelled to be quite crowded. Raymond became aware he was the 5th corpse on his mound, as he watched more mounds be assembled down his aisle stretching all the way to the door. The sheer number of deceased in his trailer alone troubled Raymond. Not because each of these frozen mummies used to be a walking-talking loved one or anything. And not because he felt it sad the virus was ravaging a good amount of folks. If you could believe it, Reverend Raymond Carter was put off by so many dead because he didn't feel special.

In life, Raymond was always the center of attention. Between Meadowview Megachurch, televangelism, his social media activity on Instagram, Facebook, Twitter, and even dabbling on Christan Dating sites, Raymond enjoyed a certain level of privilege. His existence was something to behold. A thing of great envy for others. Something people looked up to and aspired to be. Raymond owed it all to God, of course, but he would be lying if he didn't admit that he more than enjoyed the attention.

He craved it. It meant as much to him as serving God. Comparative thoughts like those, Raymond did his best to keep far removed from his prayer life, but he couldn't deny their existence. It was a pretense he had adopted in an effort to keep something private from the omniscient higher power. Presently, however, the reverend felt himself not caring if God could hear his cravings or comparisons. Fear of being "found out" was replaced with grieving the life of blissful addiction that got shattered on the summit of Mount Theo.

Denial had no place in this scarlet house of horrors. Raymond didn't talk to his neighbors much anymore. He still prayed, but his prayers were slowly becoming tainted with disdain. Despite knowing those feelings to be the whispering of sin chipping away at his faith, he could not deny he felt bitter.

Bitter about God. Bitter at his confusion in this cooler. Bitter that his lights were still on without knowing why.

Why? Why me, God? What did I do to deserve this? I've thought it through many times, and every time I deduce that I should still qualify for redemption. Qualify for your love and forgiveness for my meager transgressions, for my deeds of greatness far outweigh my addiction and weakness. What is the point of power and privilege if you cannot pursue what your passions demand?

The continued silence swallowed him. A silence devoid of beating hearts and aspirating lungs. A vacuum so complete that he questioned if he had any conscious senses at all besides sight and thought.

Was I that dreadful a servant, Lord? Was I so wicked that I don't even deserve proper Biblical damnation? Instead, I'm left with—with this! This dismal abomination of existence! It is a travesty, Lord! For a servant so high as myself, I demand recognition! Acknowledgement!

I demand attention!

No voice came. No demand met.

There were no more visitors. Once the final aisle between the farthest rows of bunks was full of X-shaped piles of corpses, the nurses were filling other trailers. The mystery woman also never returned. Raymond began wondering if he had imagined her. Maybe all of this was imagined. Could all of this just be one overdone nightmare by a dead mind? What if it was just a grand finale? A hallucination between dying and death.

Raymond remembered reading a story by Ambrose Bierce called *An Occurrence at Owl Creek Bridge.* An American Civil War soldier is hanged, but before death takes him, he has a radical and profound vision of a grand escape in which he survives. It is revealed that it was, in fact, just a vision. A trick of his mind before the rope caught and his neck snapped. Could this be like that?

Raymond focused down on Theo. Dear Theo, who had remained such a motivator and beacon of normalcy for Raymond's ridiculous circumstance. Although Theo's blood-red face warped frequently into a smiling devil patronizing him, the reverend would rather have the company of a demon than of nothing at all.

What did that statement say about him? Was he so afraid to be alone with himself? Did seeking the company of others in life prevent him from looking in the mirror? Was his penance to be alone with himself?

What if it was the girls?

The question came to him subconsciously. Those social connections may be considered less-than honorable by some standards. That is why it had to be sorted out by God rather than men, after all. Only God could judge a man of Raymond's caliber and quality.

Well, at least before he died, that was the case. Now, he didn't know anymore. Raymond let his mind slip to one of those encounters. It was worth analyzing the past since, for the time being, he didn't seem to have a future.

The last woman the reverend was with before he died was named Tracy Jones. Tracy subscribed to the Meadowview Megachurch Instagram page in December 2019. Raymond maintained the church's Instagram page (which he did for all the megachurch's social media accounts despite his already busy schedule) and Tracy immediately caught his attention. She was everything he typically sought in his bottomless thirst for special satisfaction.

Tracy had short, dark brown hair and mesmerizing gray eyes. She was 20 years old, had a dazzling figure for a girl her age, and most important of all, she was in search of answers. Tracy was struggling emotionally due to a nasty relationship with her father back when she was a teenager. Despite him being a devout Christian man, he was prone to bouts of anger and frequently lashed out at his family. Under his tyrannical rule, Tracy rebelled. To spite her father, she began seeking refuge with a group of misfits at school in Houston. That quickly led to her experimenting with different types of drugs.

After dropping out of school, Tracy had been sent off to rehab so she could find her way. When she was released a year later, Tracy was 18 years old and trying to follow the new way she had found. Like most rehab centers, the therapy was oriented around forming a relationship with God to defeat the afflictions of addiction. After 2 years of freedom from rehab and wrestling with which church to attend, Tracy decided to look into the most successful church in Houston. This led directly to Reverend Raymond Carter.

Following her subscription to his church's Instagram, Raymond reached out to Tracy. He thanked her for her interest in Meadowview and encouraged her to watch the live broadcast of his sermon on the upcoming Sunday. The beauty of televangelism is you don't have to attend the church physically. You could learn, take part, and receive the message wherever you are.

Impressed by his prompt attention to her, Tracy did just that. She watched him preach on a Sunday in January and loved it. He was so welcoming and handsome. Tracy found it easy to imagine she was sitting in the front row instead of in the women's shelter she called home.

A few weeks passed. Raymond reached out after each sermon to thank her for attending. One day, he contacted her about more than the sermon. He wanted to know about her. Where did she come from? Where did she live? What were her interests and her dreams? Tracy had never had such an important man ask her anything like that before. It made her feel special.

She told him everything. A couple of weeks later, they were video chatting about her life and God's path for her. They talked several times a week. Not for long, usually, but it wasn't the amount of time that kept Tracy excited about it. It was the quality of the talks. How charming and knowledgeable the reverend was, and it was refreshing that he really wasn't that old.

During one of their video chats, Raymond had asked her if she would like to meet for private sessions where they could talk about her future. Tracy was ecstatic, and of course she would.

He invited her to his private residence in River Oaks. Tracy understood that he didn't want to meet at Meadowview due to the sheer number of people that come-and-go. To make things even easier, he would send a car for her.

Send a car he did, and climb in, she had. Tracy arrived at the grandest mansion she had ever seen. Raymond walked right out the front door to her and offered her a hug. After their initial meeting, Raymond led her around to the back of the property to climb into a golf cart. The corner of the property with his private study was across the grounds. It was much too far to walk—he assured her. They laughed together, and away they went.

The mentoring study was extravagant. Most of the furnishings were made of dark wood and covered in leather. Large tapestries and paintings of Biblical stories adorned the walls. Books lined every shelf from ceiling to floor wherever they would fit. The space was full, but not cluttered. A fire was already lit, filling the room with the scent of cedar and warmth. The environment was disarming, elegant, and comfortable. Tracy relaxed easily, like most women Raymond brought there.

It hadn't taken long during their lesson for Raymond to bring up her living situation. How unfortunate it was that life had presented such a raw deal for her at such a young age. As a budding adult, she needed something to fill the gaps created by her misfortune. Tracy lamented she had no ideas about how to improve her work and living situation. Working at Starbucks and slowly getting on her feet was the current plan.

Raymond had smiled at her, a full smile accompanied by warm walnut-colored eyes. When he suggested that he had an opportunity for her, she was taken aback. Not outraged or upset, but unsure. The job was simple: go back to the halfway house and Starbucks to recruit women around her age for Meadowview Megachurch. Encourage them to look into the church and take that first step by watching a sermon or attending a meeting. He would pay her handsomely for her help in extending his flock.

This was a practiced dance for Reverend Raymond Carter. It usually went about the same way each time, with minor subtleties that varied between individual girls. The dance started with his mission for them. His assignment. The work. After the mission was revealed, he would talk about opportunity and gratitude. How lucky he was to have found such a lovely girl for God to work through. He had never encountered someone so unique, so special to partner with in pursuing his mission.

This was an immortal bond the two of them shared. A bond so real, he could feel it between them. He was thankful beyond words that she was a blessing in his life. Out of everyone out there, God had led her to him to help him grow his church. He had finally found his soulmate.

Their meeting was not mere chance, but divine design.

Before long, he convinced her their union would be holy. She let him unbutton her blouse, and her guard followed suit. Another bargain struck, amongst their other dealings. Raymond Carter saw this as God's work. Spreading the gospel while enjoying the fruits of his labor as a successful bachelor and businessman of the Lord. It was precisely why he never married. He enjoyed the recruiting process far too much to let it go.

His girlfriends were of age. He broke no pact of God or man in his dealings. The women benefitted in multiple ways, and so did he. They walked away richer financially, spiritually, and sexually. It was only kept hidden because it was unorthodox. Most people in his congregation couldn't live that way for countless reasons, the majority of them being financial or committal. Raymond was married in one way and one way only: to God. The flock were merely his sheep, and he led them where he thought best for them. Best for them and best for God.

That was the first time he had met with Tracy Jones. He saw her often in the following months, as he did others. The last time he met with Tracy was a mere 2 weeks before he took ill. Living that life felt like an eternity ago.

A life in which he mattered. A life in which he helped people achieve their goals while they worked within God's plan. Raymond looked down to Theo at his feet. He let the scarlet-lit towering bunks and piles of the dead fill as much of his vision as he could. That old life was over. Conquests of spirit, business, and sex were things of the living.

What he would give to live just one more day in that life again! One more day as a 43-year-old multi-millionaire preacher of the most successful church in the world. God's best avatar on planet Earth. Now? Now his sermons never made it from his lifeless lips to the dead ears of those around him.

In resignation, Raymond reached out to God as he had thousands of times before.

How long must I wait, Lord? Will you ever come for me? Am I ever to be free again?

Chapter Seven

On the 338th day in the crimson freezer, someone opened the door. It was the first time in over 7 months. Rage at his predicament had melted into a cold bitterness for all things. Raymond truly wondered if maybe this was a glitch of chemicals in his body. There was no doubt he had died, but he doubted what was real and what might play on repeat, like the needle on a vinyl record stubbornly gripped by an unyielding bur in the trough of a groove.

Sunlight pouring in through the entrance of the pop-up morgue proved that the hallucination of his post-life existence remained fluid. It had been so long with no movement in his vision that he had accepted it may never change. That his sight and reality were as frozen as the many bodies in the blood-red light. Then, one day, the door *clicked* and opened. The red fog of reality got replaced by a harsh white light.

A form moved through the doorway and stood defiantly, casting a stark shadow against the partially illuminated gloom. Looking at it, Raymond had the first positive thought he'd had in an exceedingly long time. He tried focusing harder on the form. It was difficult, like his vision was tired or under-stimulated. *Could it be—an angel?*

No... surely not. I dare not hope. Could it be?

It wasn't. The form took a few steps out of the harshness of the light and looked down at the aisle full of criss-crossed bodies.

It was the mysterious woman. Today she wore blue overalls over a black shirt and a dark ball-cap. Raymond believed she wasn't real. That he had imagined the entire incident. But there she was, looking down his aisle before moving deeper into the trailer and inspecting the neighboring one.

Raymond's anxiety rose in a good way. He felt something that he'd forgotten how to feel. He was excited. Had she come to take him away at last? How—how could she get to him? Dead people blocked the path down the aisle. People rested frozen as thick as slabs of ice stacked 5 folks high. How could she ever reach him?

Raymond's mind was racing. He had to do something. What could he do? He thought about trying to force his body to wiggle violently. Maybe he could topple Mount Theo to get her attention. It had been so long since he tried to move; he had a strange hope inside of him. Maybe it would work this time—just maybe.

Summoning all of his will, Raymond commanded his central nervous system to send signals to his muscles, just like when he was alive. He sent the commands and alas—

Nothing happened.

Raymond yelled a curse throughout his mind. *Oh, God. I'm so—OH to hell with it! Move, damn you, move!*

Sending the signals again, Raymond fiercely tried to move. Again, nothing.

God-dang it!

Sadly, it was useless. He was dead alright. Just as dead as he was almost a year ago when he died. Dead. Dead. Dead. Lousy, stupid dead.

Turning back the way she came, the woman strode towards the doorway. Raymond imagined he was sitting up, waving his arms back and forth. Just before she reached the light, he put every once of energy he had into trying to yell at her.

Surprisingly, she stopped. Eyebrows furrowed, looking down his aisle, her eyes landed on him. She looked at his face, her eyes searched around him for a moment. She smirked, shook her head, and rushed out, closing the door behind her. The familiar red lights popped on.

Oh, c'mon! Raymond lamented. *I thought I had her for a second... Could she have heard me? Ghost stories have to come from somewhere, I suppose. Crap. Well now, she's—*

Suddenly, the trailer lurched forward. The crisscross stack of bodies at the head of his aisle tumbled over to the floor. Fear flashed through Raymond's mind as his piled up neighbors nearly toppled Mount Theo. It made him wish he could hold on to something. He didn't want to end up on the floor. Worse, facedown on the floor. Just imagining it made him shudder on the inside.

Raymond pictured spending the same amount of time staring at the darkness of a floorboard for as long as he had watched nothing happen in the red light. The thought brought him tremendous fear. He pushed it from his mind. He needed to focus on the current situation, not a pretend one.

How could the trailer move? *Wait... he thought. It's a* rolling *morgue, isn't it? So for us to lurch forward like that could only mean...*

The trailer jumped, jostling all the bodies. Bunks swung like pendulums hanging from the ceiling on metal rings all which-a-way. Metal on metal squealed under the dead weight of the swinging. His own mound of corpses bounced awkwardly. He saw the others in front of him jerk abruptly as well. Thankfully, the bumps subsided, but the locomotion of the trailer was unmistakable.

Someone is driving us, Theo! Where in the hell would they be taking us? Are we going to the funeral home at long last?

Theo remained silent. Raymond couldn't blame him, he was near speechless himself. Something was happening. He might not be in a caravan ascending to Heaven just yet, but rumbling somewhere felt like forward progress. As nerve-wracking as it was to have no idea where they were headed, it felt good to imagine different scenery. Perhaps a funeral home to prepare their bodies for rest. Maybe that was why he remained inside his head? Maybe he was not *at rest* yet.

The mystery woman had come through for him one way or another. They were on a different path. *Thank you, God. Forgive me for all the swearing today. I think you of all people can understand that I am under a great deal of stress lately. It is fair to say that I haven't been my usual self.*

Sending off his first prayer in weeks, possibly months, Raymond settled in mentally to prepare for what was to come. He hoped he got a gentle undertaker. Being able to feel gentleness or not was beside the point. He desired gentle out of principal and respect. Praise God.

Chapter Eight

Covid's dead lay strewn about the floor. Body extremities in full icy rigor jutted out from beneath disheveled death sheets. The macabre scene resembled a red-cast set in a Hitchcock film. Raymond was beyond thankful that Theo and his pile merely sat lop-sided against the nearest bunk on Raymond's left.

In front of him, in her bunk, he could see more of Magda's face than he'd ever seen before. Her sheet fell enough that her face, one arm, and a breast were visible. Raymond wished he could have kept the image of how she looked to his imagination. The truth of her grimace in death was horrifying. It looked like she was screaming. His mind created a vision in which she was calling out to him. Screaming for him as she reached for aid with her outstretched claw. The unseeing eyes were wide; her skin clung tight to her boney structure, like she had no muscle at all underneath her inflexible leather.

Tearing his focus from her, he saw Theo. His head hung back grotesquely, like his neck failed to hold it upright. His body had shifted in transit, making him appear headless from Raymond's vantage point. Pete's body had shifted as well, and his head dropped over the side of his bunk, similar to Theo. The difference was Pete was glaring straight at Raymond upside down. Instead of a disgusting grimace like Magda, he was smiling. That smirk burned its mark into Raymond. It burned and burned, scarring his mind's eye.

Raymond searched for anyone he recognized. Any of the personalities he invented to stave off the eternal monotony of madness. Magda had warped into a monster. Theo looked headless. Pete was a mask of cheer that gave Raymond more terror than comfort. Jonas remained a simple left arm hanging in the air near Magda's banshee impression. Raymond had never seen a demon before, but if he had to imagine one, he figured it would look like Magda in the torturous red illumination.

When the latch *clicked* and his prison door opened, Raymond wanted to gasp in relief. The brutish red light lifted, vanquished. Light from outside cast all the faces into shadowed silhouettes. People stepped into the trailer, talking.

"So how many do we have here?" a man's voice said with a Texas drawl. He led the way, wearing blue jeans, brown cowboy boots, and a black cowboy hat that matched his dark shirt. Twisting, black tattoos covered his bare arms.

"Each one of these stiffy trailers at Houston Methodist Hospital has 3 rows of 3 column bunks 4 bodies deep, just like you see here." The mystery woman pointed an arm at the towering bunks on both sides of Raymond, then kept walking to show the 3rd. "Both aisles have 4 stacks of bodies stacked 5 high. So, each stiffy trailer is about—" she paused as she counted quietly on her right hand. "About 76 stiffies if they are all stocked the same."

She had on different clothes than when she looked at him before the trailer lurched forward and sent all the dead vibrating around haphazard-like. They must have been driving for more than a day. Now, she wore jeans and a white halter-top with the word *Covid-preneur* written in cursive rhinestones across the front.

"Holy heck!" came a response from a man in the rear, following her inside. "Haw many them dang thangs they got over there in 'Ouston?"

The words were all slurred together, and the H seemed to disappear from his speech when he said Houston. His stained wife beater crept up around his furry beer gut. A dark rat-tail braid hung behind a green baseball cap.

To Raymond's displeasure, the man's jeans looked to be caked with old blood.

"Countless," the woman said to him. She turned her focus back to the man in the dark cowboy hat. "There are multiple parking lots full of them. How some Houston hospitals dealt with the hospital bed vacancy crisis last year is proving to be quite the gold mine. With the deal I worked out withem?" She smiled wickedly. "We could be in business for a long, long time together. As long as you can do the processing, I can do the supplyin'. What do you think?"

The man's eyebrows went up as he whistled. "Countless trailers with 'bout 75 skins a haul? Jesus Christ, Barb. That's incredible!" The man spit in his hand and offered it out to her. "You got a crew to help unload 'em all or do you just do the drivin'?"

Her grin shifted from wicked to proud. "Oh, I got the boys. You say the word—" she said, slamming her hand into his spit-slimed palm. "—and I'll make the call. Get all these stiffies hauled out for ya before two beeps from a roadrunner."

Raymond wondered what language these heathens were speaking in. Stiffies? Beeps of a roadrunner? Skins? What on God's green earth were they talking about? He thought about the comments about the trailers.

Countless. There are multiple parking lots full. The woman, Barb, had said.

Had Raymond any feeling in his spine, a chill would have trickled down it. Something told him that this probably wasn't a funeral home, and that Barb was probably not an angel.

Chapter Nine

They had arrived at a facility out in the middle of a desert. The bodies were unloaded by men that piled out of white cargo vans and took orders from Barb. When it was Raymond's turn, he was appalled at the reality of what was happening.

He didn't understand how this had become the fate of the deceased in a morgue at a hospital. Covid or not, it didn't make sense. As they were unloaded, Raymond got the lay of the land. The men were arriving two wheelbarrows at a time. Two men would walk in the trailer dressed like they were clearing out a garage. One would grab a body by the feet and another by the shoulders, and they would toss them—yes, toss them!—into a big plastic green wheelbarrow. The kind of wheelbarrow one might see at a shopping mall meant for rubbish bags with the black plastic wheels. When the pile was enough for an overflowing load of bodies, the wheel man would turn and take them towards the facility across a dirt parking lot. The next wheel man would step up to the plate and the process would repeat itself. Raymond was fortunate enough to be flopped facedown towards the top of a pile, his arms and head sticking out of the side of the wheelbarrow so he could see.

He was in the middle of nowhere. Nothing could be seen for miles and miles around except mountains far in one direction. Which direction, Raymond could not deduce. The glaring sun was bright compared to the chilled low-light cooler he had grown accustomed to. Frigid mist was rising off the wheelbarrow of corpses in the hot spring air. Ahead of them was a large warehouse of undulating metal that resembled a car garage. Raymond didn't see any cars. Then he got a glimpse of where he was going. The thought skipped a few beats before congealing into a digestive piece of data he could process.

One of the goons with a wheelbarrow was parked near a series of dumpsters in the shade on the garage side of the warehouse. The containers lined up several across, and there were multiple rows within a rectangular chain-link fence. A nugget of fear began to manifest within Raymond. He knew that if the wheelbarrows were getting unloaded into garbage bins, his fate was clear. His mind struggled to take it in. The pill was too fat to swallow. That budding root of fear grew within him. Grew such that it displaced the logic he had established while in the cooler. While he struggled with what he was witnessing, two of the men heaved one of the corpses into a dumpster without ceremony or consideration.

After the first, another. And then another. Raymond didn't understand what he was seeing. He didn't understand what type of facility this was. His mind didn't have a chance to piece it together before his own wheelbarrow pulled up in front of a bin.

"I can't believe this is a thing," the man who was pushing Raymond's wheelbarrow said. "Pretty easy money, if you ask me."

The other man walking with the load of corpses adjusted his gloves over his sweaty hands in the heat. His red t-shirt showing signs of perspiration sweating through at his armpits and around his collar. "All the same, I didn't ask you."

The first man cackled in response. "Jesus Christ, Whitaker. I'm just tryin' to make conversation." Raising up a flap of his worn flannel shirt, he retrieved his own gloves from behind his belt and put them on. "I ain't been doing this gig as long as you. I'm still sort of flabbergasted at the whole thing. I just didn't know there was a business like this out there at all. Pretty crazy, you know?"

Whitaker glanced up at the sun as it rose higher in the sky, then looked at his blabby friend. "Bobby, look, I don't mean to be rude, but it isn't getting any cooler out here no time soon. I just want to dump these stiffs, get our pay, and get back to the city. I introduced you to Barb 'cause I knew you've been hard up since you got laid off from the Luxor last year. No offense, but I don't really want to spend the day talkin' about making money. I'd rather just earn it. Ya feel me?"

"Damn. You're all business out here, ain't ya? Alright, fine. I'll shut up. Do you prefer to take the shoulders or the feet when you toss 'em?" Bobby asked.

"I don't rightly care, Bobby. I prefer them in the dumpster. I don't put too much thought into it, to be honest." Whitaker said.

"Alright, fine. Remind me not to bother you at work again. Sheesh." Bobby took hold of the feet belonging to the body next to Raymond.

"By the way," Whitaker said as he took the shoulders. "I wouldn't take your gloves off between wheelin' and tossin'. They're dead bodies, Bobby. From a Covid exhausted hospital. If you go home touchin' on your family at night, I reckon you should keep them gloves on all day. Period. I don't take'em off until the end of the day. I don't even eat lunch out here. I assume it's just crawlin' with nasty stuff."

Bobby got a serious look on his face as they hefted the body off the pile. "That's a good tip, Whitaker. See? That's all I want, man. I just want to learn how you do and how this works. It's my first day, for Christ's sake! Cut me some slack." Raymond noticed the body they held was Magda. That awful silent scream seemed to focus directly on him. Then she was airborne as the men tossed her into the container. A resounding hollow *thump* followed when she hit the bottom.

"I feel like I've been in a bad mood for over a year," Whitaker said. "My bad, man. Ever since Covid started last spring, I've been a little messed in the head. I'll try to ease up on ya." He reached for Raymond's shoulders. Taking hold, he rolled Raymond over on his back.

Bobby took hold of Raymond's feet. "It's cool. We've all had a wacked up 12 or 13 months. I understand."

A troubling thought bolted through Raymond. He had been on the top of the pile with Theo beneath him. Then, on top of the load of bodies in the wheelbarrow. Magda had just vanished into a nearly empty dumpster. She was on the bottom, and he was next.

Oh no, Raymond began thinking. *Oh please, no.* Bobby and Whitaker started swinging Raymond as they counted together.

"1, 2..." *Oh God, please not the bottom. I don't want to be on the—"*

"3!" the two men shouted together, and Raymond was airborne. It seemed as soon as he touched the air, he crashed butt first into the dumpster. His lower back had smashed into Magda's face, his head and shoulders were against the bottom of the bin. Raymond looked up at the sky. The angle was poor, but he found himself staring at the rim of the dumpster framing the open blue sky.

He tried screaming for Bobby and Whitaker, but it was no use. When was he going to stop trying to get the attention of the living? Did he hear them say 13 months? Was he in the cooler for more than a year? What job were they even hired to do? Just move bodies? One of them had mentioned the Luxor. This warehouse must be close to Las Vegas. Raymond suddenly wished he could ask the men more about what this facility did and why the morgue was being unloaded here. Where was the profit in storing bodies from a hospital in outdoor dumpsters? How? Why?

Raymond's train of thought derailed when a flying corpse fell from the sky and onto his face. He didn't get a chance to see who it might be before it clumsily landed atop him. Thankfully, it shifted and rolled to the side. Its feet were near his face, but they weren't blocking his view. He could still see.

The jubilation from that small victory didn't last. An old man he didn't recognize corkscrewed into his vision. Before Raymond knew it, the man's bloated, thawing belly was smothering his face. The visible world went black for Raymond. One of the earliest fears he had encountered after dying was rekindled. Despite being able to see after death, yet unable to move, now he was stuck in darkness with no solution. Stuck at the bottom of a growing bin of year old corpses thawing somewhere outside of Las Vegas.

As the sound of more dead continued to rain above him, Raymond lost all resolve. Any strategy he'd developed to cope with his existence in the cooler was melting away. The madness he was so afraid of reared its ghastly head. Inside of his mind, despair swallowed him in the smothering darkness.

Chapter Ten

It became clear to Raymond when the sun was high in the sky or dipped below the horizon based on the sounds that he heard. During the day, the sound of trucks coming and going would occupy his mind. Men walking and talking, Barb barking orders. Occasionally, he could hear commands in a deep Texas drawl from the man in the dark cowboy hat. All the while, Incubus' hit album Make Yourself blasted on repeat as they worked. Day in and day out, metallic vibrations and vocals from Incubus acted as a numbing gel in the background of his horror story. Raymond got accustomed to these sounds and was almost thankful for the music, even if it was far removed from the hymns and gospel worship tracks he preferred when alive. The only confusing sound amongst the rest was the spraying.

A consistent spraying and splashing sound that felt out of place in relation to the others. A truck would drive in somewhat close. Then he would hear hydraulics and the sound of metal-on-metal, an awful *squealing* sound that raked him with the desire to plug his dead ears. After the gut wrenching *squeal*, a large and fat, rolling *flip-and-flop* sound would follow. It sounded like what Raymond imagined up-ending a container full of sea life into the dust might sound like. A gross and chunky, rolling belch that raised his anxiety every time he heard it. Following the fleshy, slap-n-flop would be the sound of the spraying.

Time churned by with the cacophony of noises blended together during the day. When the washing machine of sound was over, the silence was heavenly. It was the only solace he had in the darkness of the dead man's swollen gut. To calm his overthinking, Raymond imagined the desert sprawled out as far as he could see under the cloak of night. Radiating stars peppering the dark sky, their brilliance illuminating the dust as purples and lavenders to the human eye. He thought of how the cool evening air might feel on his skin. How it would smell. Thinking of his current location beneath uncounted dead that had been thawing in the heat for days made him discard the thoughts of smell and move on to a different meditation. Raymond instead thought about the creatures of the desert night. Scurrying and rambling about looking for food and resources. Critters like rodents, arachnids, beetles, and birds. The paling thought appeared that they must be looking for this very facility to assist his bin-mates and him in decomposition...

The train of thought depressed him. Raymond wondered again where God was in all this. Should he bother praying tonight, perhaps? Could tonight be different than any other night or any other time previously that he prayed? It felt so dismal. He was starting to forget what it was like to move. The simplicity of having free will over the most basic of trifles. Simply change your environment if you are uncomfortable. Merely entertain yourself if you are bored. Send a text message when you are lonely.

Reverend Raymond Carter did, however, remember what it felt like to crave. He still craved, even in death. *That* had not vanished or escaped him. How could he possibly think of needing attention at a time like this? Why would he *want* attention at a juncture like this?

There was no telling how his body was aging in this state outside of the freezer. It was likely having a rough go of it. He had just imagined all the critters of the desert that forage at night. Also, the smell of thawing dead meat in the arid heat. None of these ruminations felt positive or made him think someone would want to witness it. Much less a young woman.

The racket of an approaching engine tore his thoughts from his woes. It was disorienting to see nothing but darkness and require ambient noise to deduce what time it must be. Raymond thought the night had just begun not too long ago, and now it was already morning again. Maybe time was moving faster than he realized. Perhaps he was getting used to being dead and entertaining himself.

Soon, the familiar echoing in the dumpster from the noises of the day was upon him. Motors starting and stopping. Tires crunching throughout the parking lot and around his bin. And of course, some- one finally cued Incubus to join the workday. The first track of Make Yourself twanged its way across the desert. The first terrible squeal of metal-on-metal surprised him with its proximity. It sounded—it sounded right next to him this time. It had never been that close before. When the squeal stopped, a whirring sound replaced it, then the gooping and slopping sound of fish flopping dead onto pavement followed.

That had also never been so close before. Now it sounded like wa- termelons on pavement. Had there been pavement he didn't notice? Raymond had little time to view the surroundings on his wheelbarrow trip to his garbage bin. Everything happened so fast. The sound of things being dragged came afterwards. It sounded sort of like dragging sandbags or heavy sacks across a hard surface.

A voice rang out through the noise. "Yup, that's it boys! Gettem' all lined up like so! Just like I've been showin' ya the past few days!" It was the Texas drawl with the cowboy hat. "We wantem' close enough together to be efficient, but far enough apart to gettem' good and thawed out."

After the dragging ceased, the spraying began. A chill ran through Raymond's psyche. An engine started up next to his dumpster. The driver reversed and was adjusting to a new position. This time, Raymond didn't just hear the squeal of metal-on-metal. He saw it in his vision. The vibrating of his container shook the dead slob on top of him enough that little patches of light appeared in his view.

Thoughts swarmed his head. He was both excited about change and hopelessly anxious about what was to come next. The mechanical whirring had begun, and the bin vibrated as it got lifted from the dust.

"C'mon now, let's gettem' all sprawled out here, just like the others. Barb's bringing a new shipment tomorrow. We gotta get a move on to keep this gravy train steamin' ahead! Let's go!" roared the Texas drawl. At his command, the whirring changed pitch and suddenly Raymond was tilting.

At first, it was a relief. The great blob blocking his sight rolled off of him as the bodies shifted. Raymond saw light peeking into his view. His face was free for the first time in days. He wanted to be excited about that. Raymond wanted to accept the relief he felt, but soon after his line of sight was free, he and the other corpses started rolling.

A sickening *flip-flip-flop* as the dead rolled out of the dumpster ended with a sloppy, dull *thwump* when they hit the pavement. Raymond's world was spinning as he rolled and rolled, and then *flapped* like a hunk of skin-covered lumber filled with sludge. When the world stopped spinning, Raymond wished he was still laying in darkness daydreaming about midnight in a picturesque wasteland. Witnessing his fate firsthand was beyond troubling.

Gloved hands eagerly grabbed for the tumbling bodies. Taking hold of any point of contact they could and dragging them away, their skin bloodying as they grated against the rough surface of the terrace. A set of hands clasped Raymond by the feet and started pulling him in the same direction as the others. The chaos and sudden jostling made him dizzy. He thought he would probably be sick if he *could* have gotten sick.

After the man dropped his feet, a bearded face with a red bandana tight around his mouth and chin leaned over him. Sweat dripped from the man's eyebrows and fell on Raymond. He had blue eyes and what looked to be matted, curly red hair. As soon as he appeared, he stood, bringing Raymond's torso up with him. He spun Raymond around and propped him up against the wall. Raymond's body popped and made uncomfortable creaking sounds as the man positioned him against a low wall that led up to the platform the warehouse stood on. It was then he got to see his dumpster and its contents plastered all over the hot, wet concrete.

The terrace itself was covered in streaks of blood, skin, and gore from various sources. The machine Raymond heard every day was a forklift that lifted the dumpsters and overturned them onto the pavement behind the warehouse. Once dumped, the bodies were hauled abrasively into position with their backs against the platform wall by the workmen. As corpses were dragged, they left sloughed off skin and tissue behind them. Trails of blood, like person-wide tire marks, covered the concrete. A single drain was located in the center of the patio. Chunks of flesh and grotesque plugs of coagulated blood lay caught in the drain's maw.

Raymond truly couldn't look away. Between the shock of what he was taking in and the inability to avert his eyes, the scene of naked bodies from the morgue dumped from a garbage bin and grated against the patio had his mind boggled. This was an utter madness he had never wanted to bear witness to. Proof God had abandoned him. There was no mistaking that now. Heaven wasn't coming. There would be no ascension. Whatever this hell was that had found him, this was it. This was his reality. The afterlife was a junkyard of terrible things that a mind couldn't fathom. Wasn't equipped to comprehend. To make matters worse? Raymond had never felt so alone. He hadn't even seen Theo since he was unloaded from the trailer. Two men walking over with fire hoses caught his attention.

Besides it being arid and mid-morning, with the sun bearing down on the living and the dead, the pavement was soaking wet. It was then that Raymond remembered. The spraying. Why did they need spraying?

"Alright boys," said the Texas drawl, wearing a black cowboy hat. "Lettem have it. Let's thaw these stiffies out so they can go to process-ing!"

Processing? Raymond thought. *What are we getting processed—into? God, I'm so sorry I corrupted your sacred ways, oh Lord. If I can be freed from this, I am ready to repent for any wrong I did. Surely I provoked your wrath and must be taught. I am listening, Lord God. Please!*

God remained silent. One of the men pulled a wide lever on the nozzle of his fire hose and a beam of water punched forth. The blast was powerful enough to knock all debris off the body, but weak enough not to strip the skin and muscle from the bones. The water treatment must be to assist in thawing the formerly frozen corpses quickly and efficiently. But thawing them for what, Raymond didn't know.

The water was stripping some of the skin and meat from his bin-mates, nevertheless. Raymond noticed the amount of tissue blast-ed off the bodies. A river of chunky red flowed from the base of the wall towards the central drain, where flies buzzed around the trapped bounty. Several of the men stood by and watched, along with the Texas man in his cowboy hat chewing a toothpick. The album Make Yourself finished the last track and started over with the first song: Privilege.

Raymond waited in horror for it to be his turn. Waited for his Privilege.

Chapter Eleven

At the peak of anxiety, as his neighbor got mauled by the two men with pressure washers, Raymond prepared himself for what was coming. He figured he wouldn't feel any pain, but the thought of being washed so abrasively—of his body being damaged by the brutality of the water—bothered him somewhere deep. A deep place that light had never found, and he didn't enjoy this visceral experience illuminating that place. It felt like a violation of his humanity. The twin spears of water starting shifting away from his neighbor.

Oh God. Oh God. Oh GOD! Raymond's mind was racing. Was this going to hurt? He hadn't felt anything since he died, besides emotions. Was this going to be different? *Oh Lord, please. Please spare me this! Let me—die already! Let. Me. Die!* As the water moved closer, Raymond braced his mind against the violation of his flesh.

"Gary. Gary! Stop the water! Stop the water!" A fat man from the sidelines came running towards them, his belly bouncing underneath his white t-shirt, riding it up, revealing a Covid beer gut. "Guys, hold on!"

Both hoses stopped. The man with the curly red mane that lifted him earlier turned his attention to the approaching runner, his hose at ease, pointed towards the ground. His chisel-bodied comrade-in-arms with spikey blonde hair let his attention fall on the runner as well. Both sprayers were doused in water, staining their light-colored shirts pink from the splashing gore. The red-haired man spoke.

"What the hell, Dave? What's up? Something wrong?" Gary glanced at the muscled blonde man who shrugged his shoulders. Both looked back towards Dave. Dave stopped in front of them. His hands rested on his knees as he heaved while catching his breath. When he rose, he had a lop-sided grin on his red face.

"Ya'll don't recognize this dude?" Dave said. The sprayers looked at each other again and back at Dave. Confused looks furrowed one's eyebrows and drew the others' together.

"Ugh," the blonde man said. "Are we supposed to?" He spoke in a charismatic voice, like he should have been working in Hollywood instead of a southern Nevada desert.

Dave beamed. "Are you two knuckleheads for real? That's freakin' Raymond Carter! Like, *Reverend* Raymond Carter? Barb mentioned she spotted 'em on the trailer. Dudes, that is *totally* Raymond Carter!"

Raymond perked up (mentally, of course), listening. He thought of the mystery woman who raised his sheet the first day she stepped into the trailer so, so long ago. He remembered how she smirked at him the day she hitched the trailer and drove them across state lines. Raymond's panic was diminishing a bit.

"Raymond Carter?" Gary said. He looked at his brick-house colleague. "Raymond Carter?" Gary repeated. "You ever heard of a Raymond Carter, John?"

John turned his hose and bulk towards the next stiff in the lineup. Scrunching his face together like he was deep in thought, John scratched the stubble on the side of his head with a grimy gloved hand. "I mean, he does look a little familiar, I guess."

"You two are full of sand!" Dave exclaimed. "The famous televangelist guy from Houston! Reverend Raymond Carter! My wife is crazy about this guy. They talked about him on the news last year. He kept his giant church open during the pandemic. Thought God would protect him and he was too young to die from Covid. Blah, blah, blah. C'mon! You guys gotta remember. He got interviewed and everything. And then he caught it and died!"

Gary turned now, his attention piqued. "You know what, Dave. I do recognize this guy. Holy cow. I think my wife has a few of his books. Woah."

A smile cracked on John's face. "So, this dude is big famous? Kind of a big deal, huh?"

The drawl with the cowboy hat started walking towards the three men while he looked at his watch. Dave started nodding vigorously.

"He's a *huge* deal! Makes me wonder if we got extra for 'em." Dave turned. The cowboy hat was nearly to them. "Yo, Boss, did we get extra payment for this preacher guy? C'mon, tell us that we got extra!"

The boss spit a stream of brown tobacco spittle from his mouth to the bloody, wet pavement. A sly grin forming on his mouth. "Nope. Probably nothing extra. He's just another dead body. Barb said she recognized him immediately, and let me know we had him. I wasn't going to mention it to you fellas. She didn't say if she liked him much or not. Lord knows my wife watches his sermons. Silly old lady."

Bending his knees, he sat on his heels to avoid getting any of the sanguine mire on his expensive jeans. He looked hard at Raymond. "Shame. I wasn't a fan of his, but I hate to see a good God fearing man fall to the likes of Covid. Damn shame." Standing up, he took the hose from chiseled blond John.

Hope bloomed within the deep place inside of Raymond. It seemed he may be spared after all. He loved hearing how many of the women associated with these men endeared him. A swell of pride warmed his psyche. *God hasn't left me. God is here with me right now. This was just a trial in his complex plan for me. This might not even be the real world. Maybe all of this was just a test of my faith. My ticket to Heaven. I just needed to remain positive and trust in God. Praise his name.*

"Shame or not," the boss said. "I've never taken too kind to lowlifes that mess with young girls. You guys hear the rumors runnin' around after he died? All those members of his congregation that joined just 'cause they were part of his weird sexy web?"

What? What rumors? His panic started boiling up from the depths.

"Right, right!" Dave said. "That's why it's so wild to see him here! I thought we was lucky to get ahold of him! I'm takin' a selfie with 'em before we hosem down. My wife'll get a big kick outta this. Is that okay, boss?"

The boss nodded. "Don't bother me none. He weren't no pedo, but he was running Meadowview Megachurch like a dang brothel. A special brothel. One just for him and for chicks my daughters' ages. It was disgusting and predatory, is what it was. Treating his congregation and status like some kind of pyramid scheme to creep on girls and make more money by growing his followers. Christianity turned cult, if ya ask me."

"So you believe he did all that?" Dave asked. "Me and my wife were talkin' about it just the other day. She doesn't believe it. She thinks them girls are just after his money now that he's dead."

"Wouldn't surprise me none," John added.

"Me neither," Gary agreed.

The boss looked down at Reverend Raymond Carter. "Welp, whether it's true or not, I know what I believe. I say," the boss released the safety on the fire hose, it *clicked* open.

No! That's not how it was at all! Raymond was reeling. His panic welled up as a flood, threatening to drown him. *That's not how it was at all! God, preserve me!*

The boss continued. "I say we give him some special treatment in honor of all those girls he *procured* for God and his own coffers. Selfish son-of-a-snake. He isn't going to get chopped and sold out like a normal stiff. We're gonna have some fun with him instead."

"Oh, yeah?" "Heck yeah!" "I'm into it. Waste him!" the three men exclaimed in an aggregate voice.

"Gettem boss!" Dave encouraged.

"That's right, Dave." the boss said.

Chopped and sold? Raymond was too frazzled to be confused. What kind of fun were they talking about? What in God's clean spirit were these sacrilegious, hoodwink, country-bumpkin fools doing? They had it all wrong. Besides, how could things possibly get any worse—

"Waste 'em." Pulling the throttle back all the way, a powerful jet of water slammed Reverend Raymond Carter's center mass. Flesh exploded and flapped. The skin of his chest split and filled with water, ballooning outward. Rips formed at the base of the rapidly expanding pockets, and water streamed from them like a sprinkler. The other three men started jeering and shouting. As the hose moved down, then moved up, Raymond's body was breaking down and moving in crimson, visceral purple, and fascial white rivers of refuse. Raising the pressurized beam of destructive erosion, the boss focused the nozzle on Raymond's face.

Water exploded through every orifice. His cheeks, throat, and sinuses ruptured from the power of being forcibly stretched beyond capacity. Raymond's mind was blank. Nothing could be processed past the tidal wave of reality. The laughing and cheering of the men existed for Raymond no longer. Incubus singing and twanging in the background melted away, as did the flesh from his body. All that remained was the unrelenting flood.

Chapter Twelve

It was a particularly cold winter's day in Houston, Texas that year. Social media in 2017 excavated a movement from a decade earlier, highlighting sexual abuse, misconduct, and survivorship. Everywhere you turned, there was another accusation. Accusations were being sent out like text messages against powerful men. In some cases, the men weren't even very important or powerful. Sometimes it was clear they were guilty. A gymnastics coach or military commanding officer had attempted to make the problem disappear. Some allegations appeared not to bother them anymore than swatting at a gnat. Simply trying to keep the buzz down, and the repercussions far away from themselves or their respective institutions.

Reverend Raymond Carter found himself in just that sort of predicament on that brisk autumn day. He sat in a well-lit room at a conference table a dozen stories up in downtown Houston. He and his team of lawyers sat across the table from seven young women and their legal council. The women ranged between the ages of 19 to 31. Nearly identical packets of papers lay in front of each woman. One had refused the paperwork and intended to continue her legal pursuit against Raymond Carter and Meadowview Megachurch. The rest were content with accepting a settlement in return for going about their lives without further contact with Raymond Carter.

The woman refusing the reverend's generous donation towards her peace of mind was Amanda Goode. At the time of this meeting, Amanda Goode was 25 years old. Her chief complaint against the reverend primarily mirrored the other women's complaints against him, but she wasn't satisfied with a monetary settlement to pacify her experience. She actually wanted him to face the consequences of his actions. She wanted him to step down as head of his church, make a public statement outing himself as someone who coerced women to have sex with him while they did his bidding, and she demanded some form of list be constructed of how many young women within his congregation or otherwise were involved in his deviant behavior. In this matter, Amanda Goode and Raymond Carter disagreed profoundly.

These seven women shared a similar account in the accusation that Reverend Raymond Carter of Meadowview Megachurch used them for sex in a pyramid scheme to grow his followers, both in faith and on social media. The women claimed the relationships were coerced in the sense that they thought they were monogamous and special in nature. Like the reverend and they were beginning an actual courtship, and it wasn't just about sex and finances. They were also upset that all the female family, friends, and associates of a specific age range that they introduced to the church at the request of the reverend were also approached in the same manner to have sex with him and recruit yet more young women to the congregation, and so on.

Raymond saw this differently. He defended that the young women, all of legal age mind you, consented to a quid pro quo where they offered themselves physically in exchange for his mentorship, guidance, and, of course, his money. Many of them enjoyed a higher standard of living than they could previously afford through the agreed upon financial compensation Raymond offered each and every one of them.

Although considered poor taste in some circles, the sex was consensual, and they recruited other women as he requested out of their own free will.

With the rekindling of the social media movement to highlight sexual survivors, these seven women felt violated enough to confront Raymond Carter personally about his behavior and how they felt about it. For most of them, it had been many years prior. Only a couple of the young ladies had physical relations with Raymond within a year or so ago. Amanda Goode, for example, hadn't had sex with Raymond in nearly 6 years. The oldest of the women hadn't slept with him in a decade. Nevertheless, the movement had gotten them all thinking, and then talking, and now confronting the reverend together. He handled it with a wide smile and a casual demeanor.

Raymond Carter knew they were just confused and doing what was popular at the time. Since the settlements included the women discontinue all posting on social media regarding the reverend and cease dragging his name, faith, and megachurch through the mud, he wasn't upset about the circumstances at all. He felt no shame in the accusations. His congregation was vocal about finding the allegations preposterous and openly demonstrated their faith in him, Meadowview Megachurch, and God. Besides, he had enough money to make everybody happy again, and he was willing to share it with the people necessary to make this little spike of misguided social justice go away.

Everybody except Amanda Goode, it seemed. She continued to wage war against his name and make her demands. His church, family, and friends all understood his side of the story and prayed for her to be more humble as she found her way. They felt sorry for her, but not because they believed she was wronged as much as hoping she would one day accept God's plan for her.

After a couple of years as the movement fizzled out, fewer and fewer people followed Amanda's message online. Her campaign lost public interest and eventually, it all blew over and was forgotten amongst more current news. Social justice trends change like the wind, as they do, and Raymond continued his business of growing his church, preaching the gospel, and enjoying the affections of young women. Nothing changed for him. His routine, image, and position with followers both at church and online remained—for lack of a better word—godly.

Reverend Raymond Carter's life was as good as it could get. He wanted nothing more. Living his life as a wealthy bachelor ahead of the biggest church in the nation and helping people realize God's love for them made him untouchable. The only thing he wanted beyond this holy continuance for the rest of his days was his eventual reward in Heaven. He had no idea that after his death, Amanda Goode would go online and rekindle the firestorm she tried to start while he was still alive. And this time, it took hold and garnered more than six other women and passing interest.

Raymond reflected on these things laying in a heap outside in the scorching dust with the sun high overhead. Chained up to a rusted out old Ford truck that looked like it hadn't moved since the war in Vietnam, he watched the world go by. Over the course of the last several weeks, Raymond had gotten the gist of what this facility was about and his role in it. He'd had nothing better to do but pay attention and watch the events unfold after that day when those men destroyed his body with water.

The term Raymond heard his processors use was called body dealing. Body dealers apparently buy bodies from funeral homes during normal times. Bodies that have low-income families. The undertaker might offer a 'free cremation'. The family likewise thinks that sounds pretty good, and they sign a paper stating so. That's when the funeral home sells your loved one to a body dealer. And a team of guys out in a desert at an unregulated facility process your loved one. A medical institution then purchases it to practice human trials on.

Most of the bodies that accompanied Raymond to this warehouse were thawed and cleaned much more gently than he had been. After they were cleaned, he and the rest were carried into the warehouse and organized on countless shiny metal tables. Buyers would come representing every drug company you have ever heard of to purchase parts—yes, not entire bodies necessarily, but select parts—to take back to their lab and run clinical trials on. As Raymond figured, there was a reasonable amount of money in chopping up preserved bodies and hocking them to the highest bidder. And this wasn't even a black market. This was entirely legal.

The representatives were body buyers for medical firms. Thus, the dead body chopper-uppers were called body dealers.

Barb—his *angel*—was a body prospector. A body prospector! A person who drives around the country looking for fresh, well-preserved corpses she could acquire so she could sell them to a body dealer so they could process them and sell them chop shop-style to doctors. Raymond heard it all in the daily snickering, tomfoolery, and misanthropy these goons talked about on the job all the time.

They loved discussing their problems and how they ended up here, of all places, doing this to earn a buck. This was better than slaughterhouses, they said. The pay was better, hours shorter, and it was more humane—more humane!—because the stiffies are already dead!

Raymond was beside himself with the bloody truth as it unfolded before him. Covid had been excellent for body dealers. They're making a killing. Raymond's hospital—Houston Methodist—was selling their Covid dead to this facility for who knows how much money.

Raymond wasn't really sure what happened to funerals, but they must have been deemed illegal during Covid. He sure as heck didn't ever see a funeral. He was sent to the pop-up morgue with Theo and Magda and the rest when they didn't know what to do with them. And then they sold them to this place.

When the buyers came, they told Raymond's handlers that his body had been too badly destroyed by their little pressure washer stunt. So his body wasn't in good enough condition to be purchased. He wasn't sure if that was a blessing or a curse, but that meant he was now worthless to the body buyers. It was then he learned it was Amanda Goode that made true on her quest to see Raymond get consequences for how she felt.

The buyers would ask, "What on earth happened to this one?"

His processors would reply, "Don't you remember last year when that super rich preacher out in Houston died keeping his megachurch open? Yeah, yeah, that one that wrote all the books and broadcasted his sermons on TV? Yawp, that's him. That Amanda Goode lady came out that he wasn't the godly he led on that he was. Then all them other women came forward. Turns out, this guy got with half of Houston's youth and made money on it! Corrupt, sick, middle-aged white guy. Well, we got our time withem!"

Raymond heard different tellings of the same story from the workers. The boss would talk about it most frequently. Said he didn't mind losing the investment it took to purchase Raymond, because it was worth taking out his rage for what Raymond did on his dead body. The boss said that Raymond Carter's image was ruined in the eyes of the nation. Even Meadowview Megachurch had turned on him.

Turns out after his congregation learned of how Raymond was growing the church and what he was doing with a large amount of daughters, sisters, young mothers, privileged, and needy women alike, their faith had limits. Everything Raymond built was seized by the state, liquidated, and divvied out in damages to those women.

When it became clear that no drug company wanted Raymond, his handlers walked him outside and set him down next to this truck decaying in the sun. The end result of the aqua assault left Reverend Raymond Carter with so little skin, such little muscle and meat and organs, that he was deemed unusable as a commodity. His broken and mutilated body was set to rot in the arid heat where he figured he would slowly become desert jerky.

Animals came by to have their ways with him, finishing off what the water treatment started. Vultures by day and rodents by night would pick and chew and gnaw and claw at him. At least the buzzards would just squabble over him during the day. They weren't as bad as the blasted rodents.

In the early days, he would frequently be dragged away from his spot by the Ford and fought over by the giant desert rats. His handlers would come out every morning and find him splayed every which-a-way, pick him up and carry him back to the old Ford. Eventually, they got sick of retrieving him daily and locked him to the truck with a chain around his rib cage. After the animals scavenged everything worth eating, he just sat here. With his body getting blasted by sand and bleached in the sun daily, it wasn't long before only a skeleton remained.

Raymond had witnessed many trailer loads of bodies come in, get wheeled into dumpsters, dumped onto the terrace, and hosed down. After that, they were gathered up and prepared for the meat market inside the warehouse. He never saw anyone else get the treatment that he did with the hoses. That had been his experience and his experience only. He wondered again if any of the other corpses were alive inside their heads like he was.

Wondered if any of the dozens of other people he saw processed were inside themselves, screaming at the outrage of their reality. If they were present for their limbs being hacked off and purchased for experimental drug trials, not suitable for the living. Raymond didn't know. All Raymond knew was that his life was feeling more and more meaningless than it ever had before. Perhaps this was punishment. Perhaps he had been more wrong in his life than he realized, and God truly was demonstrating that.

He certainly had nothing but time to contemplate. Contemplate, wait, and reflect. Raymond likely wouldn't spend his time praying. He was out of prayers.

Chapter Thirteen

Summer passed. Autumn fell upon Raymond's desert landscape in almost unnoticeable dullness. There were no trees or shrubs in his view, nor could he feel the air grow colder each night. But he noticed the sunrise grow lazy, and arrive later. Sunset also seemed to greet him sooner each day.

Business slowed down at the body dealership. Raymond couldn't begin to understand why. He also didn't care. The workers' attire shifting into fall jackets and thermal gloves confirmed his suspicion of the seasonal change. Incubus no longer played in the background of the macabre facility. Either they had grown tired of the album or someone shut it down. Now it was just dead quiet. The sound of machinery, the water hoses, and trucks moving about were the mainstay in stimulation for the one out by the old Ford. The one forgotten.

This is how time ground by. Raymond practically counting the minutes between sunrise and sunset daily. He enjoyed watching insects meander by. He had also grown fond of watching birds. Thankfully, he had no more bounty worth investigating for animals. They left him alone for the most part. Occasionally, he served as a perch for a flyer or a hydrant for a canine. Most of the time, though, he sat alone and undisturbed.

Forgotten. Forgotten and forsaken. Praise God.

One night, something changed. Lights approached from the distance. They looked like headlights. Raymond thought that odd. In all the months he had been watching the body dealership and its surrounding desert, he had never seen a vehicle visit during the night.

It pulled up to the dusty parking lot. It looked to be a cargo van of sorts. He couldn't tell the color, just not white. When the engine died, so did the lights. There were no exterior lights at the warehouse. Raymond wondered if there was even a security gate or fence of any kind at the end of the driveway. He'd never had a reason to think of that before now. It was a fairly simple, primitive facility. There was little to no infrastructure besides the dumpsters and the pressure washers. Three doors opened and people stepped out.

By Raymond's estimation, he and his Ford were about 90 feet from the warehouse. He couldn't see the visitors very well, but he could tell they looked sort of small. They had lighter builds and were not as burly as the men he was used to seeing around the work site.

As he watched, fascinated by the change from monotony, he realized they looked like kids. Clearly not children, per se, but young. Since someone drove, probably high school kids. They creeped around mischievously, snickering to one another and looking into windows.

Raymond wondered how a bunch of kids would find out about a place like this. Maybe a father or uncle worked here and spoke about it, not that it really mattered. Here they were, regardless. One youth unfolded his arm at the wrist, doubling it in size. It shined metallically in the gibbous moonlight, like a cylindrical beacon against the gloomy backdrop of the warehouse grounds.

It wasn't an arm at all, but a bat. A baseball bat.

Another of the youths removed a backpack and set it on the cold dust. Two of them knelt at the backpack, pulling out clinking bottles that didn't sound empty. They gathered a few more items from the bag, but Raymond couldn't make out what they were. The snickering between them started again. Snickering that didn't sound like boys. Raymond had assumed it was a group of boys, up to no good in the middle of the night. It became apparent the two standing up with the backpack were girls from their voices.

All of them were dressed similarly in dark pants and sweatshirts. One of the girls had on a white hoodie, the other two wore darker colored tops that didn't show up in the moonlight. The kid with the bat took out a flashlight and shined it through a window. After looking in, they hurried to the next window, shining the light in again. They must have found what they were looking for, because they turned and called to the girls.

"Hey, yo, check it out. Get over here." The one with the bat was male.

One of the girls shouldered the backpack, and they both made their way over to him.

"Seriously? What do you see?" one of them asked.

"Hella dead bodies, bro! Omg," the boy said. "Look at all of them. That's crazy, right?"

"Wow. They're actually here. I almost didn't believe it," the girl with the backpack said. Both girls were holding a couple of bottles each. Raymond couldn't tell what was in them.

This would be an odd place to come drink as teenagers, he thought. The girls crowded the boy, looking in the window, his flashlight bouncing around the inside of the building.

"How totally weird," the girl in white said. "Yeah, I didn't expect there to actually be dead people inside. I thought like, body bags and stuff or something, but not just mother truckers laying on tables. That's so—gross."

"I think it's perfect," the girl with the backpack said. "This will hit 'em where it hurts. Should be quite the show."

That statement gave Raymond pause. *A show? What's the plan? Drinking and making out with the deceased in proximity? Kids are getting weirder and weirder. A direct result of social media and not enough church, no doubt.* At the thought of church, Raymond felt a twinge of sadness. He didn't enjoy thinking about church anymore. He let the train of thought go to watch the teenagers.

"Do you think it changes anything that they're all inside?" the boy asked. "I didn't expect them to like, actually be inside. I thought they'd be in coolers or something. Not just—lying around in there."

"Heck no! It doesn't change anything!" the girl with the backpack said. "If anything, I say it's better this way."

The flashlight flickered as the boy looked around the vicinity. It stopped on the girl with two bottles and the backpack. "Alright. I'm still down if you two are down then," he said.

"I'm still down," the girl in white said. "No lie."

"Definitely down," the other said. "Go for it, Trav."

"Yeah, Trav. Get it!" echoed the girl in white.

It looked like a big grin spread on the boy's face, and he handed the flashlight to the girl in white. Both girls backed up as he gripped the bat with both hands. In that instant, Raymond knew they weren't here for kiddy make-out games or fun with a ouija board.

Rearing back, the boy took a swing. The window shattered with a sharp echo and Raymond heard it bounce back off the mountains in the distance. Both girls cheered.

"Woohoo, Trav!" "Get it, bro!"

Trav inserted the bat through the window and forcibly traced the edge, breaking the sharp glass as it passed. He stalked to the next window and smashed that one in, too. A light suddenly pulsed near the girls. A light, like a candle flame, danced to life, illuminating a circular bloom in the darkness. The girl with the backpack held out the lighter for the other, who passed one of the bottles over the flame. It ignited, quickly.

Fire? What would they want fire for? It all clicked together for Raymond before the action took place. Using the existing flame off of her comrade's bottle, the girl with the backpack lit one of her bottles as well.

They wouldn't, would they? Surely they know better than to—

The girl in white let out a piercing, whooping howl. Backpack girl joined her, followed by the boy, who ran to a third window and smashed it in with the baseball bat.

"Heck, yeah!" the girl with the backpack howled, and then she threw her flaming bottle into the warehouse. Like she was waiting for permission, the girl in white followed suit, hurling her fiery cocktail through the same window.

"Trav, you wanna do one?" one of them called.

"Of course I do!" he replied, running back to the girls in excitement. The girl with the backpack handed him a bottle.

Raymond watched in shock. They had looked inside. They had seen all the bodies in there. Human bodies. They didn't care? What was the matter with these kids? Weren't they worried about getting in trouble?

With the rag atop his bottle lit, the boy ran back over to one of the windows, throwing the fire bomb in like a baseball. The explosion inside roared as it joined the existing inferno. They all lit a second bottle each and circled the building, hurling in yet more fire cocktails. They yelled and hollered and yowled the whole time, like it was a ritual of sorts.

The fire rose high into the sky. Raymond could only imagine the stink that must have been permeating the air. He was silently thankful that he couldn't smell it. Burning colors of red, orange, yellow, and amber pulsed, eliminating the night. The three youths all stood back as the flames and heat grew in intensity. They watched as if in awe of what they had done, mesmerized.

It was crazy for Raymond to think that they weren't afraid of being caught. But when he thought about it, he had no idea how close or far he was to anything. There were no visible city lights at night. No sounds of a highway close by at all. So, maybe this was truly the middle of nowhere like it felt. He thought of how dumb the boss of this operation must be to not have some form of security or anything out here. Something stupid like this was bound to happen, eventually.

He watched as the facility was utterly consumed by fire. The desert burned the brilliant colors of conflagration, turning the gloom into a scene of brimstone and destruction. Everything glowed in the artificial sunlight. Raymond decided it was almost beautiful. Poetic, really. This is how his life felt most of the time. Burned to ashes. Rendered to its lowest and most consumed state. Here he was, a skeleton in the midst of what he always imagined could be a scene from Hell. The Hell he was no closer to than he was to Heaven.

"Yo, what is that?" the boy asked.

"Just one of those classic old Fords. My uncle has one just like it," one of the girls said.

"No, no, not the truck," he continued, taking a few steps towards Raymond. "The skeleton."

Chapter Fourteen

"Do you think it's real?" the girl in white asked.

Oh, no.

"Woah, dude. He's like, tied up over here away from the body farm," Trav said. "What do you think the story is, Kelsey? Why would those creeps tie this guy over here away from the farm?"

The girl with the backpack stepped closer to Raymond and knelt in front of him. The fire reflecting off her eyes made her look like a demon as she looked him up and down. She had black, straight hair with gothic, doll-like makeup. The way she looked at him made Raymond extremely uncomfortable. He remembered what happened the last time a woman took a special attention to him. The memory of Barb still haunted him.

Barb reminded him of the water. The spraying. The men laughing as they debrided his flesh right from his body. It made him want to tremble, but he couldn't. Fire would be bad, too.

Please don't light me on fire. Please?

"Maybe he was going to expose the creeps that run the farm. Maybe he was one of the good guys. Tortured and killed to keep their gross secret from the world," Kelsey said.

"Probably," the girl in white agreed. Now that she was closer, Raymond could see she had blonde hair in pigtails, and heavy eye makeup. "How do you think they killed him?"

Trav stepped closer, kneeling next to Kelsey. "He's got literally like, no skin left on him. Look, even his organs are gone! That's crazy. What if they like, boiled him in acid like in those serial killer movies? Or skinned him alive and fed him to animals before he died."

"Ew. That's—gross, Travis," the blonde girl stated.

"Jesus Christ, Travis," Kelsey said. "You're freaking Ariana out. Get your mind out of the gutter. They probably just tied him up out here to starve and rot in the heat while he had to watch them farm the bodies he wanted to save." She stood up, hiking the backpack higher on her shoulders. She looked at Travis. "You're proof boys pretty much just think of sex and cutting people up. Probably at the same time. Freakin' A."

"Freakin' A! She's probably right," Ariana added. "Which definitely isn't hot, Trav."

"Yeah, definitely not hot," Kelsey confirmed.

Travis stood up, facing off against the girls. "Whatever. You two just like to gang up on me. When ya gonna make it fun and just have a three-way? If you're going to give me so much crap, I might as well get something out of it."

Kelsey smiled and rolled her eyes. "*Literally* in your dreams, Travis. Never gonna happen." She looked back down at Raymond. "I like to think he died honorably. I guarantee the body farmers killed him, though."

"I bet so, too," Ariana said. "Aw, crap," she said, turning away from Raymond and the other two.

"What?" Travis asked.

"I think I hear sirens," she said. "It's hard to tell if those are blue and red lights coming this way with the farm burning. They are, aren't they?"

"I think they are," Travis said. "We should probably get the heck outta here. Even if it isn't cops, fire trucks would call the cops after they arrive." He started walking away. Ariana followed him.

"Wait," Kelsey said. Travis and Ariana turned around. "We should take him."

What? Take me...

"Are you insane?" Travis blurted out. "No. Absolutely not. I'm not touching that nasty thing. Literally, who knows where it has been!"

"Don't be such a pansy." Kelsey turned and looked at Raymond again. "We know where he's been. He's been right here and probably died trying to put the body farmers out of business. We should honor him."

She looked back at her friends. "My van, my rules. C'mon, help me get these chains off of him. I have an idea for him. We can't let the cops or firefighters have him. They'll probably just cremate him and not think anything about it ever again."

Ariana jumped into action with Kelsey. The girls started untying the chain that held Raymond to the Ford. Travis breathed in exasperation. He looked towards the sound of sirens coming their way, then at the girls, and then back to the approaching authorities.

"Ugh. Fine! God, you two are so ridiculous sometimes," he said.

Ariana smirked over at him. "Hey, we tolerate your stupid three-way jokes. Least you can do is help us kidnap a skeleton. Only cool guys get threesomes, Trav."

"Yeah," Kelsey added. "Definitely only cool guys get threesomes." The girls laughed together as the chain slipped off of Raymond.

"Keep teasing me with it and it better happen," Travis mumbled, pulling the chain from around the axel of the truck.

"Keep dreaming," Kelsey said. "Okay, *now* let's get outta here!"

With his eyes wide and incredulity evident on his face, Travis blurted out, "You two are mental if you think I'm going to pick this dude up."

Laughing as they ran, Kelsey called back over her shoulder. "Be a cool guy Trav!"

The sound of the girls laughing faded as they ran towards the inferno to get back to the van. Travis dropped his arms in exasperated resignation. He turned to Raymond.

"You better not have diseases or something. You're getting a bath as soon as we get where we're going." Kneeling with a disgusted look on his face, Travis grabbed Raymond by his rib cage and hoisted him up onto a shoulder. Turning towards the van and the burning warehouse, Travis began speed walking away from the dilapidated old truck. It was Raymond's turn to mumble. Inside of his head, of course.

They're actually kidnapping me. Body-napping me? Corpse-snatching me? I welcome a change in scenery. That Kelsey girl is probably right. The authorities would likely just cremate me. I don't want to imagine what would become of my psyche if I was cremated...

Wherever these kids take me, it will be better than here. What happened here was like dying a second time. As long as there is nothing to do with water... anything but water.

The haunting sound of the sprayer was the last thing Raymond thought of as Travis opened the back of the van and laid him gently on the floorboard. He saw chunks of himself washing away towards the central drain. Rivers of flesh brutally separated by blades of white water. He pushed the memories from his mind.

As the kids sped away from their crime, Raymond felt relief as he watched the orange light of the flames fade away in the window and be replaced with the speckled blackness of the night sky. A change of scenery would definitely be nice.

Part II

Amicus

Chapter Fifteen

"C'mon, hurry up!" Kelsey whispered from the open doorway while she held the door open.

Travis and Ariana lumbered into the small, dank space. Each had one end of Raymond. As they stepped into the dark room, Kelsey let the screen door shut gently before rushing ahead of them and pulling a beaded string hanging from the ceiling. A single bulb on a swinging wire lit up the shed. Kelsey pointed towards a corner next to a wheelbarrow. "Just put him over there. Maybe behind some tool handles, just to make sure my mom couldn't randomly spot him if she comes in here for some reason."

Oh, great. Another wheelbarrow.

The space was cramped by a push lawnmower and numerous landscaping tools. It was wooden, as far as Raymond could tell. It must be a garage. They had only ridden in the car for about an hour. The warehouse had been far from most things, but apparently, people lived within reasonable proximity to the place. Before it got torched by teenagers, anyway. God bless these bloody teenagers.

"Yeah, yeah. I think that's good enough. You two wanna crash here tonight?" Kelsey asked.

"That's cool for me," Ariana said. "My parents are still away for the weekend. Vegas again."

Kelsey looked at Travis. When he didn't immediately reply, she raised her eyebrows. "And?"

Travis sighed heavily. "Alright, sure. I can just tell my dad our study group ran late. I doubt he'll care, anyway."

Kelsey grinned. "Cool. We can pretend to go to class until my mom leaves for work. Then we can figure out what to do with our friend here."

As they pulled the chain to kill the light, Travis blurted out, "Any chance for that threesome?"

Both girls whispered harshly in unison. "Piss off, Travis." Ariana added a "Geez. Give it a rest."

***

"I think we should, like we talked about last night." It was one of the girls' voices.

"That's going to be beyond gross," Travis said as he opened the screen door and lead the way into the garage.

"Have you never cleaned a skull or bone or anything before?" Kelsey asked. "I've collected animal bones since I was a little kid. This will be like that."

Travis scoffed. "Yeah, sure. Washing and bleaching a skeleton in a bathtub is *JUST* like that!"

Making their way over to Raymond, the kids started moving the tools around to access him.

Wash me? Why do they want to wash me? He thought about his current condition for a moment. *Okay, I understand washing me.*

Travis hoisted him up. "Ariana, a hand, dude?"

"Ugh," she groaned. "This is all you and Kelsey's idea. I don't even know why I'm still helping." She grabbed Raymond's feet while Travis kept hold of his shoulders.

"Would you two stop fussing? After we're done, you two can leave if you want. This won't take *that* long." Kelsey led the way out, propping open the screen door. Then they were carrying him up steps into a kitchen. Through the kitchen, they rounded a couple corners into a bathroom. Kelsey started running the tub.

"Lay him gently in the tub," Kelsey ordered. "I'll go grab my forensic cleaning kit from my room." She darted out of the door as the other two did as she said. As Travis and Ariana laid Raymond in the rising water—

Water? Ugh. It'll be fine. Raymond, you can do this. It isn't like the warehouse. You'll be fine. You also don't have a choice...

—Kelsey popped her head back in, making them both jump. "And wash your hands!"

"Jesus Christ," Travis shouted, almost dropping Raymond's shoulders. "That girl is on one. It's too early for her nonsense."

"Oh, shut up. You know you like it," Ariana said.

"I do not!"

"Whatever, bro. Lie to yourself all you want. I know why you tolerate her *nonsense*." Ariana winked at him.

As the water rose above Raymond's face, the two kids became blurry from the depths of the tub. Their voices were muffled, but he saw Kelsey come back in wearing teal neoprene gloves and carrying a bucket and a white plastic bottle.

Flipping off the cap, she poured in a few caps of solution from the bottle and set it aside. Travis and Ariana were bickering amongst themselves while both washing their hands together in the sink. Kelsey submerged her hands in the water and grabbed one of Raymond's hands and started scrubbing it with some sort of brush.

Raymond wasn't sure how long he was submerged in the tub. His anxieties about the water melted away as the water grew murkier from his debris. Kelsey drained the tub after the water grew too opaque to see through, then refilled it. She added another few caps of the solution and went back to scrubbing. The other two just watched and provided commentary for Kelsey's efforts.

Finally, Kelsey drained the tub a second time and sat back on her heels. Turning on the shower, she rinsed Raymond's skeleton thoroughly. Gathering her cleaning kit, she stood up and walked towards the hall.

"Whew, alright. Can you two grab a couple of those white towels and dry him off? I'll be right back," she said.

"Anything you say, highness," Travis mocked.

Ariana elbowed him. "Be nice. You could leave whenever you wanted, you know?" She grabbed a towel from the toilet seat and started patting Raymond down.

Travis scoffed at her from the sink. "Riiight. Sure I could. She hasn't been giving us honey-do lists since 6 AM this morning or anything. We could just bail whenever we want!" When Ariana didn't bother with a reply, he grabbed a towel and joined her, although notably irritated.

By the time Kelsey appeared again, she carried a laundry basket. "Is he about dry?"

"Dry enough," Ariana said. "Now what?"

Kelsey extended the hamper. "You can put those in here. I went ahead out front and got his throne ready. Bring him to my room real quick."

My throne?

"Go ahead and haul him back up. I'll get these towels going in the washer," Kelsey said. With a smirk, she added, "mommy never has to know."

When they picked him up, Travis took over alone to carry his body. Travis gripped Raymond's thighs and raised him to tote him out of the bathroom. Passing by the mirror, Raymond saw himself.

He was a polished, bleached skeleton.

It was mind blowing to see himself like this. He had no eyes. His skull was completely empty. He could see clearly through his head to the back of his cranium. That thought alone made no sense to him.

How could he see? Raymond heard Ariana make another joke at Travis about Kelsey. How could he hear them? His ears were long gone. He had no more skin or meat left anywhere on his body. Between the water treatment, the animals, his time out in the desert elements, and now polished clean by a macabre-enthused young woman in high school.

Raymond was truly shocked to behold himself. Within an instant, the mirror was gone, and Travis was lugging him through the hallway of the house. Arriving in Kelsey's room, they were greeted by a makeshift workshop on her floor. There was a large white square of Tyvek from the post office and an assortment of tools and wire.

"Just lay him down here. This is going to be the longest part of the morning," Kelsey said.

"What are you going to do to him?" Travis asked.

Travis and Ariana laid Raymond down as Kelsey requested. Kneeling next to the skeleton on the floor, Kelsey looked up at Travis. "He needs some hardware installed, that's all. If he is going to stay in good condition, that is."

Travis and Ariana exchanged looks. "Hardware?" Ariana said.

"Hardware. Right. Of course," Travis said. "Of course, there's *one* more thing. There's always one more thing with you."

Kelsey rolled her eyes and picked up a pair of wire cutters and a spool of thick taxidermy wire.

Hardware? Raymond thought.

***

Ariana held a front door open for Travis and his cargo. Kelsey was out in the front yard. As Raymond was brought forward, he saw what Kelsey had meant by his throne.

Next to a big tree with most of its autumn leaves scattered about the ground around it, there were a few stacked hay bales with pumpkins on them. Between the hay bales was a wooden rocking chair. Kelsey helped Travis put Raymond in the chair. With his new wire connections between his joints, Raymond's body was easily moved without the stiffness or breaking of sinew and old tissue. Kelsey positioned his legs crossed and both of his elbows on the armrests. Bending one of his arms, she propped his skull up in one of his hands. She stepped back to admire her work, her arms folded across her chest. Travis and Ariana stood next to her.

"Well," Kelsey started, "what do yous twos think? Pretty classy, or what?"

Travis smirked. "I mean, he looks pretty realistic. I'll give you that."

Kelsey looked at him. "I'm sure he does. But does he look *too* realistic, or does it work?"

"I think it works," Ariana said. "Why would anybody figure it was real? That would just be crazy, right?"

The three of them laughed. Kelsey spoke up, "Right, right. That would just be *C-R-A-Z-Y.*" She laughed. "I personally think he's the absolute best Halloween decoration I have ever seen."

Halloween decoration? Oh, no. So that's what time of year it is.

Travis moved between the girls and put his arms around both their shoulders. "Not bad booty for burning down that disgusting body farm, right?"

Kelsey reached up and moved his arm. It dropped away. "Totally. Eff the body farmers, man. Ever since I heard Daniel Wallace at school talking about his uncle working there? I was hella creeped out. That's just gross. I'm glad we burned it down. Good riddance."

Ariana let the arm stay. "Gross? Says the girl with an actual human skeleton in her front yard after we watched her clean it in her freaking bathtub."

Travis and Ariana laughed. Kelsey shifted her weight and just smiled at them, triumphant. After admiring their work, the kids exited stage right, talking amongst themselves. Raymond sat upon his throne in his inquisitive posture, not of his own free will. An autumn wind rustled the remaining leaves on the branches above him. A sparse collection of yellow and red foliage fell around him. His chair rocked ever so slightly.

A bloody Halloween decoration, he thought. Raymond would have shrugged if he was capable. *A welcome change of scenery. I'll take it.*

Chapter Sixteen

It wasn't so bad being a decoration. Raymond thought he could get used to this. Kelsey and her gang would come around and position him in funny, different ways every couple of days. Sometimes he'd hold a plastic knife or be caressing a pumpkin in his lap. The group of young arsons put capes, top hats, fake blood, and used a surprising amount of other props on him over the course of a few weeks to keep him festive. Travis once thought it would be funny to have Raymond holding his own head and tried to crank it off his neck. Thankfully, Kelsey was there to smack sense into him. Raymond was relieved. He didn't want his head anywhere besides where it was. He didn't welcome change to his current station. Either Heaven, Hell, or Halloween decoration. He didn't desire to experience anything new anymore.

Kelsey was an avid caregiver. Raymond had to admit, of all the different interactions he'd had thus far after his death, this dark-humored girl was by far the most gentle and caring. Whenever Ariana or Travis suggested something damaging to his skeleton, Kelsey would tell them no. The few times they had glued things to him or covered him in fake blood, Kelsey always washed it off by hand the following day. Once he was vandalized by a group of local hooligans that wrote and drew profanity all over his bones, and Kelsey was there scrubbing it off the following day. She even talked to him occasionally when the others weren't around.

Maybe it was Raymond's vanity speaking, but anyone would enjoy the comfort of a friend in his position. Actually, people appreciate kind words and affection in *any* position, don't they? Even if one was being punished by his cruel God, or if his beliefs were all a lie to begin with, it was plain to see how that person could get impossibly lonely undergoing his plight.

It didn't hurt that Kelsey was female instead of male. An attractive one for someone her age, gothic or not. Raymond admitted to himself often that he truly appreciated her. Her care of his body and bringing him to this reasonable existence would have brought tears to his sockets if he was capable. Kelsey was a single flame of solace in his bleak post-lifetime misery. Being her sentient toy really wasn't so bad.

One afternoon, a bright red big-rig truck rolled up and parked in front of Kelsey's mother's house. Raymond immediately didn't like it. It felt like an intrusion on his view. Normally in the afternoon, he would watch the neighborhood go about its daily ebbs and flows. He'd see the same few folks everyday walking their dogs after they got home from work. The occasional stroller with parents would go by, chatting about whatever was exciting or lackluster in their day-to-day lives. On especially entertaining days, he'd see a young woman run by in spandex and a sports bra. Raymond had counted four so far that ran by at pretty regular intervals during the week.

Well, not today! Not with that big, stupid thing blocking my view. What is it doing here, anyway? I've never seen any eighteen-wheelers around this neighborhood...

The driver's side door *clicked* open and swung on its hinges. Raymond waited in irritation to see this turd, who blocked his view of the street and other houses. He'd grown quite fond of it. The view, that is. He'd grown fond of it and he was in no mood to tolerate some newcomer interfering in his reasonably okay time. Bah-bloody-humbug is all Raymond had to say about that (he'd scream it at the top of his lungs if he could talk). Raymond wondered what time it must be. Kelsey would be home soon. Maybe Kelsey could get this twerp to park his diesel-guzzling-turd mobile somewhere else.

A speckled alligator leather boot emerged from the cab of the truck. Its unpolished heel landed on the steel step, and a man stood on it. A wind blew downed leaves around Raymond as his sockets feasted upon the driver. The same wind caught a dirty blonde mullet on the man, making it swell up and wave from his shoulders. His face wore a smirk of sorts, almost a snarl. A blue jean vest rested over a long sleeve shirt that matched the red hue of his truck exactly. Denim pants that matched his vest completed the ridiculous look of the man. After looking around expectantly, he stepped down from the cab.

Walking from his truck, he made his way across the lawn towards the front door of Kelsey's house. The truck driver had an irritating gait. He waddled more than walked, like he spent too much in his life riding horses, and his legs were a permanent bow-legged reminder. Spotting Raymond, he stopped in his awkward tracks. Changing direction, he waddled towards Raymond instead. His smirky-snarl warped into a lop-sided grin. Crossing his arms in front of himself, he looked Raymond up and down in his rocking chair. Today, Kelsey had him positioned with a plastic sword gripped in both hands and impaling himself in his chair. The twerp reached out and touched one of Raymond's forearm bones.

Raymond wished his skeleton could glow red with heat and burn the fool. How dare he touch him! The truck driver, ignorant of Raymond's outrage, moved Raymond's hands aside and drew the sword from his ribcage.

Raymond imagined shooting lightning bolts into him from his sockets. Lighting him up like a Halloween Christmas tree. A fleshy, burning mass of stupid and fat. He saw the lightning flash and flash and FLASH!

Alas, no lightning came. No flesh burning. Nothing of note at all.

Swinging the sword around in mock wonder, he grinned at Raymond. "Well, I'll be," he said. His voice sounded hillbilly, jubilant. Raymond found this irritating as well. In fact, everything about the creature in front of him irritated Raymond. "I didn't know Julie had gotten so into the holidays. How fun! I bet it was really Kelsey, though. Am I right?"

This line of speech confused Raymond. This buffoon knew Kelsey and her mom? But, after all the weeks that had passed since Raymond had been sitting here in the yard, he'd never seen this—thing—before. Kelsey had never mentioned him in front of friends or to him in her personal dialogues. The mullet-sporting child leaned in suddenly and wacked Raymond on the shoulder with the plastic sword.

"It was Kelsey, wasn't it ol' boy? C'mon, you know you can tell me?" he said.

I'd love to tell you to get your grimy smile away from my face and try to swallow that sword.

"Welp, I guess your secret is safe with me, ol' boy. I won't tell nobody. Ha!" With that final snort of a laugh, he rammed the sword back through Raymond's ribcage.

The jolt rocked him forward in his chair so he was staring at fallen leaves and grass instead of the waddling-child's truck. The man reared back, putting his hands on his potbelly, and belched a hearty belly laugh. Raymond imagined his breath probably smelled like fermented anchovies left in the sun, or a back-alley Chinese restaurant dumpster. He silently thanked the universe his olfactory faculties were long gone.

When the laugh was over, Raymond heard him crunching foliage to his right and continue his way towards Kelsey's front door. The door opened and slammed behind him. That goblin didn't even knock before he barged in. Raymond suddenly hoped that Kelsey and her mother weren't in danger from the husky waddle-gaited troll.

This turned out to be the first afternoon that Raymond felt sad in quite some time. Staring at the multi-colored leaves in his view, Raymond hoped Kelsey would get home to fix his position soon. It would be very good to see her today.

Chapter Seventeen

It was late into the night when Kelsey finally arrived home. Raymond remained impaled as she crunched through the leaves in the yard. She didn't stop to check on him. Kelsey walked straight past him and into the house. That's when the yelling started.

After Julia got home from work, she'd gone right inside. No mind paid to the big rig parked adjacent to her yard. Raymond heard talking and an exchange of exuberant 'hellos' between the truck driver and Julia. Raymond didn't believe in intuition, but he had a feeling Kelsey's absence was related to the arrival of this truck.

Who was this man? Was this was Kelsey's father? It hadn't occurred to Raymond in the slightest until this moment. He had trouble imagining that beast creating a treasure like Kelsey. Maybe she just had more of her mother in her.

Raymond's musing was interrupted by a loud outburst from inside the house. He heard the front door open and slam. Outcries from the fallen foliage alerted him to footfalls behind him. Someone had left the house. Oh, how he hoped it was the waddler on his way back to his machine. Maybe Kelsey had run him off.

When Kelsey arrived next to him, she sat on the ground and leaned against Raymond's tree in the center of the lawn. The man leaving would have been better, but this was the next best case. Raymond couldn't look directly at her to see what condition she was in. When she sniffled hard and he saw her dark sleeved arm wipe at her nose, he knew she was crying in silence.

Many moments passed. There was no second door slam. Neither adult followed Kelsey outside to comfort her or continue fighting with her. Raymond figured neither was better than upsetting her further. He was anxious to know what was going on. He hoped this wouldn't be one of those cases he would never fully understand, since he couldn't ask her questions directly. More and more, he learned how much of a curse his circumstance could really be. Finally, Kelsey stirred on his left.

She stood and moved in front of Raymond. Her dark hair was braided into twin pigtails. A light, long-sleeved black cardigan highlighted a collared white blouse she wore underneath it. Grabbing him by the shoulders, she pushed him back into a comfortable sitting position. Gripping the sword and pulling it free, she turned and threw the sword spinning into the red big rig.

Justice, Raymond thought. Not that the Halloween prop truly represented vengeance, but he had learned to enjoy little victories when they came. He couldn't throw the sword, so he was thankful when Kelsey could and did. It felt like more justice than Raymond had witnessed in a long time. That brought up a dark thought in him.

What if Amanda Goode would consider this justice against him?

"I'm sorry I let him mess with you. He had no right to touch you," Kelsey said. She fiddled with his hands, eventually crossing them in his lap. After crossing his heels, she changed her mind and crossed his legs instead. "I hate it when he visits."

Raymond watched her as she watched him. Kelsey looked directly at his face, like he was actually a person. It made him feel so seen. It gave him the feeling he was actually in a conversation with someone. Raymond had the illusion of talking to Theo and the gang back in the pop-up morgue, but he knew what that was. That was entertainment. Something to keep his mind occupied while it drifted endlessly at sea. Drifting at sea, patiently waiting for a shark to end it for him. He still wondered if a shark would ever come.

Who is he? Raymond wanted to ask. *Who is the brute, Kelsey?*

The thick makeup around her eyes made the whites shine and stand out in the low light. Her cheeks were puffy from the emotional outbursts he heard while she was in the house. In an abrupt change of events, she uncrossed Raymond's bones-for-legs and scooted him aside in his rocking chair. Kelsey turned and sat next to him, and slowly started rocking the chair. Pulling out her phone, she started scrolling. The screen lit up her face in the darkness.

To his surprise, music began playing softly. He knew that voice. Who was it... Ed Sheeran! Raymond was proud to have recognized the artist. Most popular music wasn't important to him when he was alive, but he was discovering he really appreciated it now that he was dead. Ed Sheeran was one of the few he liked in life. The song she played for them now was *I See Fire*. Raymond admired her pick. Putting her phone in her lap, she rocked them as they both stared ahead at the enormous truck, blocking their views.

"I see Waffle House parked his stupid truck in your way," she said. "Figures. He's about as considerate as a menstrual cycle. He just shows up whenever the heck he wants, takes what he wants, and leaves again. Typical, if you ask me."

Raymond thought Waffle House was an appropriate nickname for the goon. It seems Kelsey shared similar views to Raymond about the man. *C'mon, tell me who he is, Kelsey. Please, tell me.*

"You know, this is going to sound stupid, but I wish you could talk. I bet you'd have some really interesting things to say. Like, I'd wanna know how you died? Who were you? Were you even a man or were you a woman? I'll be honest, I haven't bothered researching how to tell the difference with just a skeleton. I thought I'd spare you the embarrassment of me checking your pelvis without asking. That's just, rude."

As Ed Sheeran's tribute to The Hobbit continued playing, Raymond was taken aback by her acknowledgement of him as a person. She didn't see him as just a body. Kelsey actually thought of him as something that used to live. The insight of this teenager who he had watched burn down a body dealership continued to amaze him.

Kelsey continued. "I'm sure your hips would tell me. Because, c'mon, we both know hips don't lie and all that. Heh." She laughed at her own joke. The laugh stopped awkwardly. Putting her hands underneath her thighs to keep warm, Kelsey shrugged and took a deep breath.

"I hope you were a better person than this guy. I mean, don't get me wrong, he isn't terrible for my mom. He doesn't like, mistreat me or her or anything gross like that—"

Good, Raymond heard himself think. Not that he could do anything in the slightest if that had been the case.

"I just really don't like him. I don't like it when he appears out of nowhere and ditches my mom for weeks, sometimes longer, and just shows back up like everything is totally fine. That's messed up, you know? You don't treat someone you love like that. That means he doesn't love her, right? He's just," Kelsey sucked a hard breath into her lungs and held it. "Using her. That's all this is to him. He's just passing through our nothing town in southern Nevada and shacking up with whoever lets him. And he's just gross on top of that. That doesn't help anything.

"And who is it that lets him? My mom. Out of everyone in town, it's *my* mom that this pig shacks up with. I hate it. I really, really hate it."

I See Fire ended, and the next track started playing on Kelsey's phone. Raymond recognized it immediately. *Photograph,* also by Mr. Sheeran.

"I don't know what kind of man—I'm still assuming you were a man—but I hope you didn't treat women like this. I hope you were better than that."

Those words broke against Raymond like a wave of arctic water. For the first time since he died, Raymond was glad he couldn't speak. He wouldn't know what to say. Had he been better, or was he just as bad as this man Kelsey described? When he was alive, he had never thought about these questions. Honestly, he never did. These weren't the types of things that held his mind's attention back then. God, faith, money, vanity, and pleasure consumed all his living cognitive abilities in life.

In death, these questions came up with surprising frequency.

Kelsey shifted her weight and looked towards him. "I'm sure you weren't a womanizer. I will admit, though, I wonder how you ended up at the body farm where me and my friends found you. That is *quite* an interesting place to end up dead and unburied. I still like to think of you as a hero that died trying to shut it down. Trying to do the right thing by all of those poor dead people.

"That's why I took you, you know. I took you because I think it's disgusting how we treat people after they die. We just," she raised her hands up in exasperation and let them drop as he looked back out at the truck, blocking most of the streetlights. "We just divide up their stuff and have to spend a ton of money to get them processed somehow. Like their death wasn't burden enough on the ones they left behind, but now they have to *deal* with the body. And those creeps making money off of the dead? It was worth risking a few years in prison to feel like I freed those people and punished the degenerates making money off of it. Off of the business of death."

Kelsey looked at him like she expected him to respond. Raymond wished that he could, but the silence dragged on. It weighed on them until Kelsey lifted it herself.

"It's messed up is all," she said, looking out into the darkness of her neighborhood. After scanning the shadows and finding nothing of note, she continued.

"I don't know why I'm getting into all of this with you. Sometimes I feel like I don't have anyone to really sit and talk with. My mom is—annoying—and distracted with her friends and her flings around town ever since her and my dad split up a couple of years ago." Kelsey raised an eyebrow and pointed at the truck with a fist and her thumb. "Trust me, this ain't the only dude that comes around my house, unfortunately. I think I just like him the least. It just sucks, you know?"

Leaning forward in the rocking chair, Kelsey put one of her Doc Martens against the ground and shuffled leaves around with the other one. Raymond wished he could interact with her. Comfort her. Validate some of her concerns and critiques of how people were treated both alive and dead. Although he was glad he wouldn't have to tell her what his relationships with women were like when he was alive. Raymond didn't think he could face that critique from this young woman in this moment. He was worried his spirit may never recover.

"It doesn't help that boys my age seriously only seem to want one thing from girls. Well, that and video games. Video games seem pretty important to them, too. I know it's cliché, but it's cliché because it's true. Even Travis." She stood, walking away a few paces before turning. "Travis and Ariana are my two best friends. I talk to them, sure, but honestly? They are both *so* obsessed with sex. She's into him, he is into anyone who talks to him. It's kind of impossible. I want to take Travis seriously as a friend, but he constantly makes jokes about hooking up.

"And the only guy I ever actually hooked up with? It totally wrecked our friendship. We were really close until we weren't. It didn't feel worth it. Besides Ariana, I really don't get along with other girls. So, I guess that leaves me with you." Kelsey kicked at nothing in particular on the ground. "I'm just the nerdy goth girl who kidnapped a skeleton from a body farm and polished it up to be her only real friend. In the space of a living amicus, I adopted a dead one."

Smiling in spite of herself, she walked up to Raymond. She put her hands on her knees and leaned in towards him. "Do you know that word? It's Latin. I've been studying Latin in school since freshmen year. I think it will give me a leg up in science classes as time goes on. Amicus means friend. Maybe that's what I'll nickname you. I have to call you something since I don't know your name. How do you like Amicus?"

I like it just fine. As an animate skeleton, Amicus feels oddly appropriate.

Kelsey continued. "Well, regardless of how stupid the world is, I'm glad I found you. Thanks for listening, even if you didn't have a choice. I actually feel a little better. Between you and Ed Sheeran, I can believe there are better men out there somewhere. And truthfully, I'm in no hurry to find one, anyway."

Kelsey stood to her full height and quickly moved around him towards the house. Raymond wasn't ready for her to go. That didn't feel like a proper good night. The fear of her going inside and leaving him to his thoughts so abruptly welled up inside him. He realized he had never heard the door and footsteps were coming back to him.

Appearing in front of him again, Kelsey picked up one of his bony hands and placed a rose in it.

"One thing my mother does right is grow flowers. I don't know how she keeps them alive this late in the season, but she manages. Here is one for you. I'll check on you in the morning. Thanks for hearing me out. Hopefully, Waffle House will be gone before I go to school. Sometimes he's only here for a few hours, sometimes a few days. I'll cross my fingers that this time it's on the shorter end. See ya in the morning, Amicus."

Raymond heard the door open softly and close even softer, and he was alone again. There was a lot on his mind after the events of tonight. Sitting with his rose in the dark, Raymond wished he could see the moon or the night sky like he could in the desert before his rescue. The moon felt like having company around when he was alone. Kelsey's words both lifted his spirits and haunted him, and they were his only company for the rest of the night.

Chapter Eighteen

"Alright, I think that will do for today. Somewhere between suave and spooky. The perfect gentleman, if ya ask me." Kelsey had stepped back to admire her work. Ariana and Travis were walking up from around the big rig parked in the street.

"Ew. Waffle House is here?" Ariana said. "Dude, I truly have *no* idea what your mom sees in that guy. It's—bizarre. For real."

Kelsey rolled her eyes and gave Raymond a 'kill me now' gesture by imitating hanging herself. She turned to face her friends. "Yup! He's in town, so I'm cool to get outta here ASAP. I'd enjoy not seeing him today before school."

Travis walked up and stood in front of Raymond. "Bringin' back the top hat and cane look, eh? Didn't you do this one a couple of weeks ago?"

Kelsey's eyebrows arched in mock shock. "I sure did. And it's a good one, so I did it again. Is that okay with you? I didn't realize I needed permission to dress my skeleton however I want."

Ariana and Travis looked at each other, then burst out in laughter together. "*Your* skeleton, Kelsey?" Travis said. "I'm sorry, I forgot. Who helped you get that skeleton?" He looked at Ariana, then back to Kelsey. "Isn't it sort of, *all* of our skeleton?"

Ariana's hand shot in the air. "I agree with Travis! *Our* skeleton." Turning towards him, they high-fived. When they noticed Kelsey wasn't laughing, they dropped their arms. Their faces and mood lost some thunder.

"Whatever. Our skeleton or not," Kelsey said, "he stays at my house. I'll dress him however I want. Besides," she continued in a defensive, but harmless tone, "I added a little vampire blood to his jaws. It isn't the *exact* same costume as before. It has—flare."

The other two teens looked relieved she wasn't actually upset. Travis beamed at her. "Totally," he said. "It's rad, Kelsey. So ugh," he pointed a finger up the street. "School?"

"Yeah," Kelsey said. "School." Walking up, she fell in line with the other two as the trio walked off the lawn and towards the road. Kelsey turned once, looking over her shoulder at Raymond. It was a look he saw on her the night before, like she looked almost as lonely as he felt.

Soon after, she went about the normal talkative state she got into when she was around her friends. Playful, yet with an air of leadership. It was a side of her he only saw when they were around. When they left, he felt he saw the real Kelsey. The one she didn't show other people.

Raymond sat alone again in his rocking chair next to hay bales and pumpkins. Fake blood smeared artfully around his teeth and dripping down his chin, and a top hat atop his skull. A black cane with a gold ferrule propped up his right hand while his left held up his chin stoically. Spooky, yet suave, Kelsey had called it. He wished he could see how he actually looked, although after thinking about it, maybe he didn't.

The one instance in the bathroom mirror as the teens carried him from the house some weeks back was quite a shock. Just because he knew his body was reduced to a skeleton didn't mean he enjoyed witnessing it firsthand. It gave him the creeps.

***

"I know, I know. I'm sorry for how she acted. I should have told her I was expecting to see you yesterday. Me dating is hard on her. She just isn't used to it yet. I hope it didn't put you off too badly."

Behind Raymond, the front door opened briefly, bringing the sound of Kelsey's mom, Julia, onto the porch. As the door closed, Raymond heard the deadbolt engage. As it did, a voice he wanted to forget responded to Julia.

"Oh, it's all good, Jules. Kids will be kids, ya know? What can ya do?" The belchy laugh Raymond heard yesterday croaked quickly. It sounded almost like a cough or a hack, more than a laugh.

"I'm so glad you understand. That's something I like about you. You're just—easy. Don't ask for much, never expect things to be perfect." Julia said. They were almost down the walkway to the driveway where Julia parked her car.

The man laughed off her observation. Raymond couldn't see them, but now their voices were to his right instead of behind him. "It's nothin', Jules. I appreciate you seeing me whenever I'm in town. I like it simple and easygoing. Most women don't understand my lifestyle. I appreciate you having your own opinion. It doesn't bother me if your daughter doesn't like me too much. I ain't datin' your daughter."

They both chuckled together. Raymond wanted to puke.

"Right. You're right!" Julia said. "Well Buck,—

Buck. Buck must be his name.

"—I've got to get going to work. Macy's doesn't run itself! How long are you going to be around this time?"

"At least a few days. My load won't be ready for a little while. More time I get with you!"

Raymond could imagine Kelsey's reaction to this news. She had been hoping he'd leave today.

Raymond heard a smooch between the two. "Okay!" Julia said. "Well, make yourself at home. I'll be home later. Try not to pay attention to Kelsey's attitude. I'll have a talk with her."

"Sounds good, Jules," Buck said. "Always appreciate your hospitality. I'll be around. Have a good day at Macy's."

"Alright, Buck. See you later." Julia opened her car door to climb in.

Buck was suddenly in Raymond's view as he waddled his tugboat figure across the yard. His head turned and looked at Raymond. He wore the same outfit as the day before when he arrived. Gator boots, red button up, mullet and all. The memory of this goblin running him through with the sword and leaving him stuck staring at the ground rose in his mind's eye.

"Hey, Jules," Buck called after her.

But it was too late. Julia's white sedan was already away from the driveway and making its way up the street. Buck walked over to Raymond, scanning him with his meatball eyes. Raymond wondered what on earth must be going on in that fleshy bowling ball Buck had for a head. Was he admiring Raymond's attire? Maybe he was a Halloween enthusiast? Worse yet, was he a bully and took pleasure in breaking things that didn't belong to him? It wasn't long before Buck's consistent gawking started bothering Raymond. Whatever the man was lingering on, Raymond had a bad feeling about it.

"I'll have to ask Kelsey about you. You intrigue me, Mr. Bones," Buck said.

I can't say that I feel the same way, Waffle House.

"You intrigue me quite a bit," he said as he turned towards his truck. "Guard the house while I'm gone. I reckon I'll be back pretty soon. Just out for a bite to eat and some errands."

Thanks for the update.

The nerve of some people, Raymond thought. As Buck's truck rumbled to life and pulled away, Raymond looked forward to the unobstructed view of the neighborhood. Although it sounded like he would see Buck again, he wasn't looking forward to it.

Chapter Nineteen

Buck came and went throughout that week, but inevitably left as promised. He continued to commit weird acts towards Raymond. For whatever reason, Buck saw him as a child's toy to be messed with. Kelsey would set him up in a costume that day, and Buck just *had* to put hands on him somehow.

It could be something as simple as tipping his hat or repositioning Raymond's limbs, but not limited to taking his cane or sword and smacking Raymond with it. Personally, Raymond thought Buck just sort of—liked him—for whatever reason. It almost seemed a compulsion for Buck to bother him.

Finally, the day came for Buck to depart. Raymond saw more of Kelsey after that. It was clear she didn't spend as much time at home when Buck was around.

Halloween was just around the corner. Raymond saw decorations peppering the lawns of the surrounding houses. It was not only a fun pastime watching families assemble festive scenes together, but it was something he felt a part of. He was himself a lawn ornament, after all.

Kelsey began confiding in 'Amicus' more and more after that first night. She would get home from school and sit in his chair and tell him about her day. Then, after the sun went down, Raymond would get an evening talk, too.

Kelsey talked to Raymond about all aspects of her life. He got to hear all about she loved science and language study. How she hated math. She told him about her dad and what he was like before Julia and him split up a couple of years back, and how much it hurt. Told him about how embarrassing it was for her mom to be dating so much.

Raymond loved listening. He felt like he was fast transforming into this name she called him: 'Amicus'. It was a word he knew from his pastoral studies. A reverend bumps into Latin from time to time if he takes Bible study seriously. No one had ever called him 'friend' in Latin before, though, and it had a fresh feeling that he enjoyed.

It was something special between just the two of them. He was her best friend. Her 'Amicus'.

When Halloween came, Kelsey dressed up as a plague doctor. It seemed fitting, since Covid-19 so recently ravaged the land. Ariana and Travis thought she should wear something 'sexier' as they put it. 'Amicus' heard all about it Halloween night after a haunted house party the teens attended. Kelsey sat with him, emotional and lamenting about how even her friends didn't really know her. They were always trying to edit something about her. Filter her.

It hurt her feelings much more than they realized. This was safe to surmise, because Kelsey told him she rarely had such honest talks with other people. Running around society as a high school girl was confusing, it seemed. She felt a lot of pressure from many directions to be something she wasn't. All she wanted was to be herself.

Her 'Amicus' was always there to perk her up after a long day. When Halloween was over, Kelsey and Julia broke down his pumpkin, hay bale, and rocking chair habitat. Kelsey wanted to bring him inside into her room. It was amazing how much Julia opposed this.

They got into an argument about it right there on the front lawn. Words like 'grow up' and 'what's the big deal' were thrown around.

Julia accused her of not letting things go and that led to the ugly territory of making this about her father leaving.

That was a misstep on Julia's part.

Kelsey yelled at her, then accused Julia of making everything about herself and her divorce. Her dating. Of putting her life ahead of Kelsey's, and how that isn't how *real* parents treat their kids.

The battle was bloody, but Kelsey eventually got her way. 'Amicus' was allowed to come inside, even after Halloween was over. Kelsey had a window seat in her room. That served as his new resting place. She continued to decorate him in fun attire long after Halloween had passed. Their talks were practically continuous whenever she was in her room and not distracted by her studies.

It was pretty clear she was an introverted girl, not easily understood by others. Raymond would have felt sorry for her, but he didn't see anything wrong with having an inanimate confidant. There didn't seem to be anything unhealthy about it, really. She was a loner. The world was filled with brilliant loners. Her core friends she kept at arm's reach were all she seemed to need. It was their expectations that were hard on her. Maybe that was why she confided in 'Amicus' so often.

Raymond, as her amicus, didn't have any expectations of her. Kelsey could be her truest self and vent to him as one would a diary. He grew to thoroughly enjoy spending time with her.

The quarrels with Julia still happened. Julia would nag Kelsey about how odd it was to talk to an object in her room. She compared it to having an imaginary friend. Kelsey would sarcastically shoot right back with something like, "Would it be better to get pregnant in high school or get addicted to drugs or get arrested at sixteen? Would you rather me do something like that instead?"

Those arguments got shorter and shorter as time carried on. He couldn't blame Julia for being concerned, but Kelsey's points were always more poignant. Nothing seemed to be wrong with the teen, after all. If anything, he thought she was possibly the most genuine and honest person he had ever met. She was a surprising sixteen-year-old. Of that, he was certain.

Winter break came and went, and a new high school semester started and ended. Raymond began to really embrace his new role with Kelsey as 'Amicus'. He caught himself identifying as 'Amicus' occasionally. One had to be flexible in an ever evolving afterlife. Forest Gump's famous line about chocolate came to mind: you never know what you're going to get.

This seemed as healthy and positive as his afterlife had gotten thus far. He had full intentions of embracing it.

Kelsey went away for a science camp for a week during summer vacation. It scared the bejesus out of him being alone in the house with Julia. He was terrified Julia would take advantage of Kelsey's time away and discard him somehow. Thankfully, she ignored him.

Raymond did, however, have to endure seeing Buck while Kelsey was gone.

Julia must have told him where Raymond hangs out these days. Sure enough, Buck had the gall to peek in Kelsey's room once and gawk from the cracked door. He was respectful enough of a teenage girl's room not to come all the way in or physically disturb Raymond's bones, but the attention was unnerving. Kelsey couldn't get home soon enough.

Time flew by with Kelsey around. It seemed only a couple of months had passed when her Junior year started. Before long, Raymond's rocking chair was placed out front and Kelsey set up pumpkins and hay bales again. She got more ambitious this year with ghosts in the trees and gravestones too. Much to Julia's dismay, Kelsey even dug little shallow graves in front of them to give the impression people were recently buried in the tiny cemetery.

Had it really been a year since Kelsey rescued him from the body dealership? He supposed so.

So be it, Amicus mused to himself. There were worse ways to spend an afterlife, he reckoned.

Chapter Twenty

One day, just before Halloween rolled around again, Buck showed up while Raymond was out front. It was bound to happen. Kelsey had dressed him up in a long red Hook costume, complete with a tricorn hat and cutlass. Just like the year before, Buck had to put hands on Raymond. He took his tricorn hat and wore it himself as he walked in the front door.

Here we go again, was all Raymond could think. Big red truck blocking his pleasant view of the neighborhood. Big dumb oaf bullying a skeleton he didn't realize was a person just trying to get through another day after they died.

People can be so ignorant sometimes.

He must have a key to the house, because he waltzed right in while Julia was at work. Kelsey got home first, of course, and as expected, was less than amused about Buck visiting. She wore black overalls today over a white t-shirt. Her dark hair was in a half ponytail. Dropping her backpack on the ground at her booted feet, she scooted Raymond over and sat down.

"I'll tell you what, Amicus," she said. "My day was honestly going pretty darn well. I knew it was too good to be true, and here we are. Waffle House is *here* in the flesh." She turned towards Raymond, her brows furrowing. "What happened to your hat?"

Stolen by flubber king.

She glanced around, looking for it in the immediate area. "If he took it, I'll get it later." Getting close to his face, she skeptically studied his skull. The edge of her mouth curled into a smirk. "I really need to work on those Amicus attack missiles already," she joked. "We've really got to work on your ability to defend yourself and the house sometime. They are clearly malfunctioning.

"Welp," she continued, "given the fact that there's an undesired buffalo inside my house—" she hopped up and snatched her back-pack from the lawn. "—I think I'll invite Trav and Ariana for some pre-cinema food. The three of us are going out tonight. Do you think the new *Jeepers Creepers: Reborn* movie will be any good, or as terrible as the first two?"

She laughed at her own joke. Something she did often. "I have a feeling it will suck just as bad, but that's half of why I like them. Well, hold down the fort. It stinks that Waffle House is here. I'll probably be home late. I despise seeing him." As she walked away, she called back, "See ya later, Amicus."

See ya later.

The worst part about Buck coming around was that Kelsey would stay away. Julia got home a bit after Kelsey left, as usual. Afternoon melted into early evening. Raymond heard the door open and close behind him. Waddling into his view, Buck appeared. He wore the same alligator skin boots as the first time Raymond had seen him, except today he wore a maroon shirt with a black velvet vest.

"So, Julia and I have been chatting," Buck said as he plopped the tricorn hat back on Raymond's skull. "She doesn't think you're a welcome addition to the household anymore. We've discussed it, and she told me if I wanted you, I can have you!"

What?

"I'm sure Kelsey won't be too happy about it, but Julia is worried about how much time she spends with you. She thinks it would be best. But that brings me to my current predicament..." His words trailed off. He was looking up at the autumn leaves still clinging to their branches, deep in thought.

She isn't allowed to give me away. I don't belong to her!

Buck scratched his head and looked over his shoulder at his truck. Jerking his head up suddenly, he ran a hand through his blonde mullet and turned back to Raymond. He wore an over-perky smile on his round meatball face. It made Raymond extremely uncomfortable.

"Oh, do I have an idea for you!" Buck exclaimed. "Yessir, yessir! Lemme see what I got in my repair kit. Oh man, do I have a fun idea!" With continued mumbling to himself about his plan, Buck speed-waddled over to his truck.

No, no. No ideas are necessary. Just get in your Piggly Wiggly mobile and get on your way.

Buck was digging through something in the passenger side floor-board. As he bent over the driver's seat, his rump stick out. His shirt and vest rode up just enough that Raymond had the pleasure of seeing that his pants didn't fully cover his plumber's crack.

Good grief. Have some dignity for God's sake. Raymond thought about him judging Buck while he sat dead and decorated by a teenage girl as a Halloween decoration. *At least I have dignity,* he thought. *I have a pirate coat and a tricorn hat.*

When Buck hopped down, he carried a small metal box. Walking the box around to the front of his big rig, he placed it on the ground. Smiling with mischief in his eyes, Buck headed across the lawn towards Raymond.

Raymond didn't like where this was going.

Buck pointed his short stumpy thumbs at himself with a duck-faced smirk. "I *love* Halloween. Love, love, love it! And you—"

Buck reached forward and snatched Raymond from the rocking chair, and slung him over his shoulder.

"—will make the coolest Halloween decoration on the road!"

On the road? Wait! Stop! Put. Me. DOWN!

Raymond was panicked. What was he supposed to do? For the first time in months, Raymond tried to move. He tried to kick violently. To buck his back fiercely. His body wouldn't respond.

Digging down deep within himself, he focused. Raymond focused all of his being, all of his mind, on the task of movement. He had moved effortlessly as a living man. Surely some spark of that was still around. It was impossible that all traces of his ability as a human were dead except for his psyche. Concentrating, Raymond lashed out with both of his legs. Commanded his arms up to smash the small of Buck's back with his bony fists.

Nothing. Despite his mental gymnastics, Buck propped him up against the grill of his truck, and turned to dig in his little metal tool box.

Please. I was happy. I have a friend. I'm Amicus, now. Don't do this, please. Don't do this!

Buck turned, holding something orange in his closed fists. "Alright, let's just take this right here—" Grabbing one of Raymond's arms, Buck lifted the wrist towards a top corner of the grill. As Buck maneuvered the sliver of orange in his fingers, Raymond realized what they were.

They were zip ties.

"That looks pretty good!" Buck said. "Okay, now over here—" Retrieving a couple more zip ties, Buck lifted Raymond's other arm to the opposite corner of the truck's large chrome grill, and zip tied the other wrist like the first.

Raymond was processing. This was all happening too fast. He wanted to call for Kelsey, to warn her. But he knew she wouldn't be home for hours. She was at the movies.

And 'Amicus' was being stolen.

With surprising dexterity, Buck zip tied both of Raymond's ankles to the lower corners of the grill. Buck leaned in close enough that Raymond thought about how his breath might reek. Buck stuck his tongue out of the corner of his mouth as he reached beneath Raymond's ribcage. With two final and quick *ZIP*s around Raymond's spine, Buck stood to his full height and backed up a couple of steps. He crossed his arms and belched a quick laugh.

"Man, oh man. I'm a genius. This is incredible. Incredible!" he self-congratulated. "I can't wait to tell the guys about this! You!" Buck leaned in and pointed a hotdog-looking finger at Raymond's face. "You are going to be the biggest hit on the road!"

Giddy with excitement, Buck left him staring down the road from the front of the truck and went inside the house. After a few minutes, Raymond heard him from the doorway. "Alright, thanks for everything, Jules! Sorry, it was such a short visit. Thanks for the companion! Happy to help!"

Crossing the yard, Buck walked around and hopped up into the driver's seat. The great mechanical beast roared to life. Raymond started vibrating viciously with the engine behind him.

Raymond couldn't think. Even if he could speak, he was speechless. He was finally comfortable with his afterlife. It was stable. Happy. He had made a friend, someone who actually cared for him. What was this madness? It made him think of the spraying. That dark time boiled up into his mind.

The helplessness of having his meat pressure-washed from his bones. The men laughing at his death and their fortune at humiliating him. Now, he was being stolen from the first kind-hearted person he had met in death. As the truck picked up speed, Raymond thought of Kelsey. The intimate conversations and inside jokes they'd accumulated over a year's time. A line from the first night she talked to him, upset, rang through his head.

I'm just the nerdy goth girl who kidnapped a skeleton from a body farm and polished it up to be her only real friend.

Her only real friend. Her Amicus.

The red semi thundered onto a two-lane highway that seemed to lead to nowhere. A long stretch of flat into unknown territory, away from his comfortable rocking chair with a pleasant caretaker. Away from *his* only real friend. When the tires hit the pavement, Buck laid onto the accelerator, and the deep rumble of the diesel engine burst to life.

Crucified on the front of the massive red beast, Raymond's mind reeled from the overwhelming sound of rushing wind.

Part III

Mr. Bones

Chapter Twenty-One

Distant landscape meandered along as they rocketed across the foreground. Concrete cut through a forlorn arid wasteland that gave way to inclines out of the dust and into the trees. Flagstaff came and went. Onward they plowed. Leaving the trees behind, they careened into the desert. Raymond saw the Arizona, New Mexico border. The truck went across it without notice or ceremony. When dusk finally crept in from the monotonous horizon, Raymond was lost inside of his mind.

His thoughts were as twisted and mangled as the ever stretching road was not. Its terrible directness to nowhere was numbing to Raymond. He wasn't sure he had ever driven from dawn until dusk, when alive. His drives covered far less distance, and usually he had a driver. Raymond would be on his phone entertaining himself while faith-talking to a young woman. Or going straight to a work event at Meadowview. Stuck in a car for a couple of hours during gridlock in Houston with the air-conditioning blasting and a distraction was nothing compared to what this was like.

Hours and hours of the constant vibration and noise of the wind and the road. Bugs of every kind plastered to his bones. Images of Kelsey passed through his thoughts, so similar to the fleeting scenery of Nowhere, New Mexico. She would appear amongst the cacophony of visual and audio stimulation, then get swept away the next moment by the squeal of brakes or the *splat* of a beetle against his skull.

In times of great loss of control, Raymond had always reflexively prayed to God. He thought of Meadowview Megachurch and everything it used to represent for him. What faith and prayer and God meant to him, and how faithless he felt now. What was the point of faith if Heaven or Hell wasn't real? The great promise of the scripture was that it all meant something in the end. That when a person's life ended, their actions and faith would be weighed, and judgement would follow. So, if this is to be his afterlife and God never greeted him, what was the point of prayer? It was like talking to a ghost.

Buck sped up and plowed over a large road alligator, bouncing the truck and jarring Raymond from his ruminations. It shocked Raymond that the man didn't dodge those things. Any normal person put on a blinker, moved around them, and safely continued their drive. Not this bow-legged fool. Buck sped up every time and barrelled over them. The man was as reckless a driver as he was ugly.

Night had at last overtaken the day when they turned off the highway and into a Pilot station for the evening. Buck climbed down from the driver's seat and walked around to evaluate his cargo. Taking a lap around the rig, he checked the trailer hitch and ensured everything looked in order. All of his rubber remained intact and hadn't joined the cemetery of tire gators he so enjoyed running over. At last, he appeared at the grill and checked Raymond's binds.

"Yup, I think my doubled-up zip ties did the trick. I don't think you moved an inch!" Buck told him.

I almost wish I had fallen off, thanks.

Buck scratched at the stubble on his cheeks. "You know, we need to call you somethin'. Even replica skeletons need names."

How can you possibly think I am made of plastic, you mutton-faced baboon?

"I've got it!" he declared, his eyes wide and his mouth hanging open like a fly trap. "When I was in high school—"

Is this going to be a long story?

"—I had this hot biology teacher, right? I wasn't ever so good at biology—"

Shocker.

"—but I remember she had one of them life-sized anatomical skeletons, just like you. She called him Mr. Bones. That's what I'm going to call you. Mr. Bones!"

Raymond wished skeletons could vomit.

Laughing at his own declaration, Buck stepped closer to Raymond. "Oh, we are going to have a TON of fun together, Mr. Bones. Just you wait and see. It's gonna be—" Buck clapped Raymond on one of his shoulders in emphasis. "—incredible. Simply incredible. Matter of fact..."

Buck reached into his pocket and retrieved his phone. "I have another good idea! You ever heard of Instagram, Mr. Bones?"

Is this ape serious? Who hasn't heard of Instagram?

"Well, we're gonna have a hashtag, just us two! I bet people will dig it! I've already got a decent following. It's kind of a lot. You'd be surprised who likes to just see me drivin' and posting sunsets with my truck."

I can't wait to hear what he considers a decent follow—

"One point two thousand. That's right! Not too shabby for a normal truck driver, huh?"

Sir, I would never insult normal with the likes of you.

"And it's already obvious what the hashtag has gotta be. C'mon, get over here."

Raymond found it ironic after telling Raymond to 'come here', Buck hurried over next to Raymond and put an arm around his shoulders. Extending his other hand, he prepared for a selfie with the sunset in the background. Buck flashed the toothiest, most lopsided smile Raymond had ever seen. Raymond, of course, couldn't pose, and continued to hang in place.

"Grin big, Mr. Bones!" Buck shouted before snapping a picture.

Standing up straight, Buck's hotdog-like fingers typed with unexpected dexterity on his phone. When he finished, he turned the screen around and showed it to Raymond. "Alright, there it is. Check it out!"

Shared on Buck's Instagram was the selfie of them in the Pilot station parking lot. The caption read:

> Got a new partner on this leg of the trip. Meet #mr-bones everyone!

Putting his phone away, Buck waddled towards the Pilot muttering to himself about how clever his idea was and how it was finally what he needed to make it big on Instagram.

Raymond hung on the grill of the dreamer's semi, feeling more numb than ever before. It wasn't from the ride in particular, nor was it because he was now Buck's captive hood ornament. Raymond was numb from the abrupt change. He already missed Kelsey dearly. Raymond wondered what her reaction was when she got home from the movies and he was missing. He imagined the terrible fight she probably had with Julia and Kelsey storming out of the house to the rocking chair with no Raymond to talk to.

Raymond vowed never to forgive Buck for taking him from Kelsey. He vowed to never enjoy anything Buck had planned for him against his will. No matter what the occasion, Raymond would mentally disobey every step of the way. The utter pointlessness of the disobedience wasn't the point.

God had abandoned him. If the boss from the body dealership was right about his megachurch, then his flock had abandoned him, too. The vow against Buck would be an effort to remain loyal to Kelsey, his only real friend in this afterlife.

Buck returned with four fully loaded hotdogs, a family sized bag of BBQ Lays, and a Big Gulp soda for dinner. After he climbed into the cab for the night, Raymond watched the moon slowly rise above the gas station. The presence of the moon didn't feel like company tonight, like it had in the past. Tonight, she only felt like loneliness.

Chapter Twenty-Two

"Alright, everybody say, Mr. Bones!" Buck said with an over-the-top clown-like voice.

"Mr. Bones!" the woman said, and Buck snapped a selfie of the two of them, posing with Raymond in the middle.

Buck had this annoying habit of saying 'everybody' when he was only referring to one or two other people. Here, Raymond figured he was really only talking to the woman he stayed with the night before. Because even if Buck was referring to Raymond as a person and encouraging him to smile, asking a skeleton you stole to smile is a big ask. From Raymond's perspective and capability, an impossible ask.

At every possible opportunity, Buck conducted this ridiculous performance. Whether it be another trucker at a Love's gas station or a random passerby in a Starbucks parking lot, he'd approach them and manage to bait them into a selfie with Raymond. It was usually followed by high-fives, handshakes, fist bumps, or back claps. And *every* time, he posted it on the Internet with a stupid comment and the hashtag he'd created. Something like this:

> #mrbones keeps rollin' east through Arkansas! Come see us on this leg of the route!

This made Raymond hope someone crazy from the Internet would stalk them and steal him away from Buck. He, of course, also went through this exercise with every woman he stayed with on the route. Such as the woman, Patricia, he'd just taken the picture with.

Based on the last few evenings, it seemed Kelsey was right in her assumption about Buck's character regarding women. Although he didn't mistreat them, calling them meaningful relationships would be a stretch. Since they left Julia's house in Nevada, they stopped in Gallup, New Mexico, where Buck stayed with a mistress named Carla. After that, Tucumcari, and her name was Kitty. Now, they were packing up to leave Patricia in Fort Smith, Arkansas.

These three encounters looked about the same as his hookup with Julia. Buck shows up, stays the night, and leaves in the morning all kissy kissy. Raymond was actually impressed that a man of Buck's appearance and demeanor could attract this many women. It had him thinking about his own rendezvous with the young women he used to pride himself on. Watching another man live loose, staying with any port in a storm, not caring too much about the wellbeing of the people involved made Raymond feel worse about how he'd behaved when he was alive.

Like Buck, Raymond didn't openly mistreat the girls he'd had relations with, but he hadn't appreciated or loved them, either. Although in his mind at the time, he was mixing business, pleasure, and faith into one experience that he relived over and over again. A combination that felt dirty now. These ruminations always brought him back to the woman who refused his payoff, Amanda Goode, and the women who didn't.

It likewise continued to weigh on his long, decayed heart that Kelsey would not love him if he were alive. She would hate him, just like she hated Buck.

The unlikely duo continued east on I-40. Raymond was unsure of their ultimate destination, but he knew well the heading. His view of the scenery and the road signs was monotonous, to say the least. He hoped the next leg of their trip would take them to prettier country-side. Oklahoma may have been the most boring state possible to drive across. There were times Raymond wished one of the tire gators Buck hit at Mach Jesus would flip the bloody truck and provide some basic entertainment. Alas, the rig ran true, and gobbled up every rubber reptile they rolled across.

Currently, they had driven most of the way through Arkansas and Raymond was seeing signs for Memphis, Tennessee. Whenever they approached a reasonably sized city, Raymond dreamt of reprieve. He craved the end of the line. The mind-numbing vibration, noise, and constant stimulation from the road made him miss sitting still. Watching the world go by was a fine way to spend the afterlife. On the front of the big rig, it simply went by too quickly. Occasionally, Raymond fantasized about Buck plowing into the back of another semi-truck, smashing Raymond's body to bits. There was no guarantee it would end his torment, but it was a welcome thought.

Reverend Raymond Carter felt like the most depressed dead person alive. From his surmisation, he'd been dead for around two and a half years, and little had changed regarding his predicament of hanging around. Crucified on the face of an eighteen wheeler thus far was his least desired way to spend conscious death. He'd almost rather get his body blown apart by water again, although he figured that wouldn't be possible. You could only lose a body once. It isn't like they grow back. Although, in his current state, Raymond would challenge what is possible or impossible had he the ability to debate.

A sign alerted Raymond to their specific location. They were about to pull onto the bridge, crossing the Mississippi River into Memphis.

It was surreal rolling over such a large bridge from his vantage point. He almost ignored the thought of the structure collapsing, plunging him, Buck, and hundreds of others into the murky water. Letting the thought go, Raymond tried to remain less nihilistic. Refocusing his attention, he took in the sights more than entertaining his dark muses.

Rising out of downtown Memphis, Raymond saw the Memphis Pyramid. He read once that this was the 7th largest pyramid in the world. Hard to believe looking at it now. Now it was just the nation's biggest Bass Pro Shop. A commercial scar on the Memphis skyline.

That made him ponder the fact he had never seen the real pyramids in Giza. He had never been to Egypt. At the current rate of things, Raymond surmised he probably never would. Soaking in the sight of the Memphis Pyramid with renewed interest, he was thankful he got to see a pyramid at all.

Chapter Twenty-Three

Buck dropped off his load at a Walmart in Memphis. Arriving at a warehouse outside of Jackson, Tennessee, Buck's truck got loaded up again, and they were back on the road immediately. Overhearing the destination was Atlanta led to peace of mind for Raymond. Although he could control nothing, it was nice to know where they were headed next.

With the trailer loaded, before leaving the warehouse, Buck rallied a dozen of the men and women working there to take a picture with Raymond. This was the first group shot the duo had taken part in. Buck insisted on getting all of their respective Instagram handles and tagged as many of them as he could. The caption beneath the post read:

> Stopped in @amazon_jackson to pick up more of your orders, folks! Here's a shot of the team and me with my mascot #mrbones! Follow us to our next stop leading up to Halloween, Savannah, Georgia!

Despite his vow against all things Buck, Raymond found himself enjoying the Tennessee countryside. The rolling hills and autumn colors were wonderful, he had to admit. Climbing up through the mountains of Nashville was stunning. He'd never seen sedimentary rock with water flowing over it before. They didn't have places like this where he grew up in Houston. Bypassing Nashville on their trip, the descent into the valley on the other side was equally breathtaking.

When they arrived in Chattanooga, Buck knew yet another gal there and parked his bright red beast at her trailer on the outskirts of town. Raymond wondered how long Buck had been a truck driver to accumulate this network of endless places to crash overnight. He wasn't sure if it was a laudable feat or more lonely than it appeared. Regardless of the truth, Buck seemed energetic and go-lucky every day. If the man was lonely, he showed no outward sign of it.

While attempting to ignore the most obnoxious lovemaking sounds he believed he had ever heard coming from the quaint brown trailer, Raymond pondered Buck's disposition on life. Maybe he wasn't a fancy or traditional man, but he wasn't negative or unhappy. He enjoyed a job that paid enough to afford the travel and truck, which Raymond always heard was an expensive endeavor for a trucker. Raymond had also never seen Buck rude, mean, or anything but kind to whoever he encountered, (excusing the kidnapping of Raymond, perhaps). Buck was friendly and talkative with anyone, seemingly indiscriminately.

In contrast, Raymond thought of his own negativity lately. Sure, his dismal mood grew from a place of fear, disappointment, boredom, loss, regret, confusion, shaken faith—a whole mess of problems with his existence these days, really. But apart from that laundry list, was it really so bad? He couldn't feel pain or anything regarding his experiences anymore. It didn't seem he was in a position to fail at anything in particular, so there were no worries there. Okay, so maybe he likewise couldn't necessarily succeed in anything either, except for changing his outlook. This opportunity for reflection could be considered a form of peace within its own right.

While he continued to let his thoughts drown out the coital racket from Buck's latest excursion, Raymond entertained the possibility of peace in this unexpected version of the afterlife. What if it was a test of his character? Wouldn't God have the power to test someone's faith to this extent? If that was the case, then why wasn't it in the Bible? Maybe that was part of the test. A *blind* test of faith.

Perhaps Buck pilfered Raymond from his loving home in Nevada for a reason. Could there still be a plan of some design in this madness meant for him, or was this truly a cosmic mistake, and Raymond was simply omitted from destiny? Floating towards nothing on an indefinite route to nowhere adrift on a sea of fate? Raymond surmised it was certainly a peculiar doom, whatever the answer was.

***

When the sun rose the following morning, Buck and—whoever (Raymond never caught the name of this one)—came out for the selfie ritual before the duo shoved off. Mouths agape, arms around Raymond's shoulders, breaths stinking, Buck recited his irritating mantra.

"Everybody say, Mr. Bones!" And then the selfie was snapped. Yet another iteration of the ritual was completed.

> Leaving #chattanooga! Buck and #mrbones will arrive in #savannah just in time for #halloween! Looking forward to bringing ya'll everything you ordered from @amazon!

An autumn rain accompanied them out of the mountains of east Tennessee and into the foothills on the way through Atlanta. Several hours later, Buck stopped at a Party City costume store on the outskirts of Savannah. Hopping down from the driver's seat, Buck waddled around in front of Raymond with a toothy grin lighting up his face.

"We've got a party to attend in Savannah, Mr. Bones. We gotta make sure we both look our best, ya hear!" Buck said in his jubilant, annoying tone of voice. "What do you want to be for Halloween?"

Raymond stared at the man. He recognized from his time with Kelsey that dressing up skeletons was apparently all the rage within some circles, but that didn't stop him from finding the rhetorical question from Buck to be fairly ludicrous.

Well, I don't know, Buck. Maybe a dinosaur. Oh, oh, I know. How about a living person? How about Kurt Vonnegut? Or David Bowie? You know, other living people, like me?

Buck smirked at Raymond with a mischievous look on his face while he shook a finger at him. "You are a stoic one, Mr. Bones. I'll pick you out something fun! Can't disappoint everyone that'll be expecting us tonight at the party." He turned and started waddling across the parking lot. Looking back over his shoulder, he shouted, "I hope you're as excited as I am!"

Esctatic, Raymond thought. He watched Buck giddily prance in his own awkward way before disappearing into the shop.

When Buck finally emerged from the costume store, Raymond was flabbergasted at what he saw. A large group of people were excitedly walking towards the truck, with Buck leading the way. It must have been the entire customer base within the busy store on Halloween day. As Buck came up to Raymond, the crowd formed a semicircle around them. Some of them hooted and hollered, others stared at

Raymond with hopeful smiles on their faces, many of them took out their phones.

Buck set down his shopping bags of goodies and put an arm around Raymond, grinning at the crowd. "This is him everybody! This is the famous Mr. Bones I've been telling all of you about!" A few of them cheered while many clapped. Phones were up and recording or snapping pictures. Buck continued.

"We're gonna be at a party tonight in downtown Savannah after I drop off my Amazon load at a warehouse. He's pretty sweet, right? I knew ya'll would love him. I can't believe some of you have heard of me and him already. That's so cool! Who wants a picture with him?"

Shouts went up from people in the crowd. "Hell yeah!" said a tall youth in the front, and he took a step forward. "I'm down!" yelled a girl, followed by a few of her friends. Before Raymond knew it, there was an informal line forming within the semicircle as people waited their turn to take a picture with Buck and Mr. Bones.

"Remember," Buck yelled over the building spectacle, "we got a hashtag! Hashtag Mr. Bones! Look us up and follow us on Insta! We'd both super appreciate it."

People assured Buck that they would. Many looked up his profile on the spot, then posed for their own selfies and pictures with Buck and his prize. Raymond didn't know what to think. He hung crucified in shock at the events happening around him. When prompted by a middle-aged couple who asked what Mr. Bone's costume would be, Buck pulled an outfit out of his goody bag and showed them with enthusiasm. Raymond couldn't believe his sockets.

In his hands, Buck presented a black and white priest's costume, complete with clerical collar and all. Buck beamed at the couple, who returned his enthusiasm.

"Don't you think that's a little morbid?" a woman in the couple asked. "A priest smeared on the front of your truck like that?"

"It's just for fun, ma'am," Buck explained. "I don't mean no disrespect by it. I just think it's funny is all!"

"I think it's awesome," a teen said, joining the conversation after taking his picture with Raymond. "You won't insult anyone. We have a sense of humor here in Savannah. And we *LOVE* Halloween! It'll be fine. Where are you and Mr. Bones going to be tonight?"

"We'll be downtown," Buck said. "Just follow along with my posts and I'll let all of you know."

"Okay, cool," the teen said.

"I suppose it is a bit ironic," the woman said. "Christianity is based on a crucified preacher rising from the dead, after all. That was very Halloween of him."

"It sure was, ma'am," said Buck. "It sure was. All in good fun here!"

All in good fun, Raymond mused. *All in good ironic fun.*

The crowd took nearly an hour to get their fill of pictures of Raymond and conversations with Buck. When it was finally clearing out, Buck looked like he'd just won the lottery. Tossing his goody bags into the passenger side of the cab, he climbed in.

All in good fun.

***

The party Buck had in mind was a car show in downtown Savannah hosted by a local Fire Department. Buck arrived dressed like a peg-legged pirate, which perfectly complemented his waddling gait. Raymond had been taken down, dressed in his clergyman's outfit, and hung back on the front of the truck. The fire engine red eighteen wheeler stood out among the classic cars at the event, but the firefighters welcomed it as a novelty.

Mr. Bones stole the show, much to Raymond's dismay. Mobs of downtown visitors in costume took countless photos with pirate Buck and priest Raymond. What started the commotion was a group of women dressed up in a series of smoldering, revealing outfits. The trending picture shown seven females draped all around the grill of the truck, Buck, and Raymond. There was a nurse, a Wonder Woman, two vampires, a Princess Leia, and two bondage police officers. Mr. Bones had a woman on each side planting a kiss on his bony cheeks, and so did Buck.

After that initial stunt, a crowd formed to watch the women. Naturally, others began wanting pictures with the duo as well, and yet more people noticed. As herd instinct kicked in, many party goers were suddenly drawn to the spectacle, and a photo-taking frenzy began that lasted for hours. Even the firefighters got in on the action. They posed with axes, hoses, oxygen tanks, and more. The firemen photo was another trend setter, both on the Internet and for passersby on the street around the event.

Buck felt like the bell of the ball, readily soaking up the attention and affection as eagerly as anyone offered it to him. Raymond remained torn about the experience. Here he hung in a knockoff clergyman costume, his skull painted with lipstick marks from a dozen different gals, his picture taken with hundreds of Savannah Halloween prowlers having a good time, and he didn't know how to feel about it.

He figured he would like the attention, so what was wrong? Why didn't this spark his craving for affection from the opposite sex and send him basking in it like his pot-bellied companion? While a couple dressed as male Thor and female Loki crossed their respective weapons in front of Raymond as Buck knelt in front, his arms outstretched dramatically, Raymond realized what it was.

These people weren't giving Raymond attention. They were giving Buck attention. Mr. Bones was just a prop to pose with. Buck was the ringleader, the figure in the forefront of the event, not Raymond. Furthermore, *Raymond Carter* wasn't at the event either. Mr. Bones was. His true identity was a mystery to all of these people. In reality, it was even worse than that. His identity didn't even exist. They thought he was just an expensive replica of the real thing. The truth would have likely disgusted them, but the joke entertained them.

As the volume of music in nearby bars rose, the car show wound down. Drivers took their cars back home, but not before they took pictures with Buck and Raymond. Buck worked out an agreement with the Fire Department to park his truck in their lot overnight, so he could go enjoy the festivities. Buck wandered off with the firefighters to a nearby party.

Hanging alone, Mr. Bones listened as the surrounding area lit up with nightlife around him. Thousands of people milled about in the busy downtown. He felt more alone than he had in a long time. At least when he was alone before Kelsey and her friends took him from the body dealership, his isolation felt more natural. Appropriate. But in the center of a party, yet unable to attend, he felt invisible.

Feeling invisible didn't make him miss Kelsey less, but he needed to reconcile that her part in his afterlife had ended. He belonged to Buck now, and letting go of Kelsey would be the strategic move to preserve what was left of his metaphorical heart. It made logical sense to accept that he was Mr. Bones now, and do his best to enjoy the ride.

Chapter Twenty-Four

Buck and #mrbones went viral the following week. Halloween in Savannah had propelled them into the spotlight on the Internet. A shocked Buck showed a silent Mr. Bones how his trucker profile on Instagram swelled from the humble twelve-hundred followers to over a hundred and ten thousand in just a week's time. With pictures and videos circulating on every social media platform, Buck took more pictures and videos to keep the momentum alive.

He started streaming live to showcase outfits he was wearing and what he dressed Mr. Bones in that day. Alerting followers about what towns were on his current route and making a point to schedule meet-and-greets became routine. After Savannah, they went to Miami. Miami was another big hit. Maybe not as big as Savannah since Halloween had come and gone, but plenty of people showed up at the beachside car show. Buck featured his bright red semi and his skeletal comrade, just like in Savannah.

When Miami's load was dropped and another acquired, they had a long haul to New York City. Buck was learning to market his videos and pictures better, and the turnout along the way to New York was surpassing his expectations. By the time the duo made it to New York City, Mr. Bones fans that wished they had been in Savannah for Halloween showed up in droves to pose with the growing sensation of Buck and Mr. Bones.

On the next leg of their adventure, Buck picked up a job that would take them all the way across the country to Grand Junction, Colorado. He made special trips to hit cities along the route. Parties erupted in Cleveland, Indianapolis, St. Louis, Kansas City, and Denver.

Weeks passed by at blinding speed, both for Buck and for Mr. Bones. He started to welcome the numbing noise of the road, because it kept away intrusive thoughts he didn't want to contemplate. Calling himself happy would be a stretch, but he wasn't miserable. Raymond had reached a place of acceptance of things he could not change. His stoicism solidified to be as constant as the expression on his skull.

The weeks turned into months as the seasons changed. Buck started driving less during the winter to focus on Mr. Bones merchandise fans could buy from his online store. Hats, t-shirts, stickers, a well designed Mr. Bones of your own, and his patented invention: the Mr. Bones Grill Attachments that hold your Mr. Bones onto the grill of your vehicle easily and securely.

By the time spring rolled around, Buck had done his truck up flashier. He wanted it easier to recognize when he attended events or when lucky fans got to see him on the road. The new look boasted a coat of royal purple paint complete with ghost flames on the big rig. Buck also embraced the showman persona by dressing in flamboyant outfits with bright colors, flashy hats, and plenty of fringe hanging anywhere it would fit. Although he kept his mullet and gator leather boots, as he insisted they were key to his image, and he would be unrecognizable without them.

Buck continued taking jobs, but at a slower rate than he had previously done. The extra income from the store and his newfound Instagram and YouTube fame enabled him to drive less and do more shows. In the spring of the following year, #mrbones had taken off so completely that the duo saw other vehicles in their travels with Buck's

Mr. Bones replica adorning their grills. Buck and the other drivers would honk noisily whenever passing each other.

On their current route together, they visited Houston. The Mr. Bones show Buck put together was across the street from a place that was familiar to the show's namesake. Raymond got to see first-hand what had befallen Meadowview Megachurch since his death. The massive building still remained, but was boarded up with a lone FOR SALE sign on the several acre lawn. A billboard high overheard, featuring the smiling portrait of who Reverend Raymond Carter had been, was defaced beyond recognition. It was clear the people of Houston had reacted in profound rejection of the megachurch's disgraced founder. This provided him the chance to consider what his life was worth to him.

His faith had proved fruitless thus far after he died. The gospel he taught for two decades may not be a lie, but what good would it do his followers after they died? If God didn't come for him, why would he welcome Raymond's former flock? The best he could hope is the thousands of souls that followed his teachings while he lived gained comfort and growth from them while they were still alive. Because after they died, Raymond could make no promises their faith would mean anything.

Enjoy the ride while it lasts, because comfort and life are fickle friends, indeed.

Enjoy the ride was his new mantra, if he bothered with one. Which made him not care how people remembered him after he died. Raymond Carter had a wonderful life and impacted many others. Millions of others. But this new mantra is what he would take with him beyond the grave. Why waste time on regrets or how people viewed or remember him? Raymond had loved his life. He loved it, and as selfish as it sounded, he didn't mind if people didn't approve of *how* he lived it.

Enjoy the ride.

Seeing the destruction of his life's work hurt, but it didn't surprise him. He couldn't have prepared any of his followers for the afterlife, because he didn't know what it would bring. From his perspective, the Bible lied to him. And maybe their afterlives will be different. Why should his experience be identical to others? What if afterlives are as uniquely suited as individual lives? What if enjoying life *is* the lesson instead of investing in faith, which is really just preparing to die? Maybe that is preparing you for the afterlife more than you realize? It makes sense. Logically, living people know as little about post-life as they do about pre-birth.

Ironically enough, he was impacting people as Mr. Bones. Mr. Bones made people smile. Helped them laugh and get together for entertaining social events. He decided he wouldn't dwell on his legacy anymore. It served no purpose in his current existence as Mr. Bones. He should embrace the ride ahead, because he had no choice in the matter, anyway. Reverend Raymond Carter was dead. Long live Mr. Bones.

Chapter Twenty-Five

Mr. Bones' second Halloween party was the first festival named in his honor. The event was scheduled for three days over Halloween weekend on a beach in Miami. Buck coordinated with the event sponsors to design colorful merchandise and branding for the concert. Banners throughout downtown and South Beach read #MRBONES in colors of the rainbow, but written in a spooky font for the holiday. Buck also got to assist in putting together the musical lineup. Names like Ed Sheeran, Miley Cyrus, The Weeknd, Incubus, Fleetwood Mac, and many other popular artists appeared on the roster.

The experience was surreal for Mr. Bones. Affixed to a display made up to look like the grill of a truck on stage, he accompanied the artists as mascot for the show. Between sets, the display was carried down to the beach so festival attendees could take pictures and videos of the novel Halloween icon. #mrbones became the number one hashtag on social media for the duration of the festival. During these three days, the vow Raymond made—refusing to enjoy anything Buck included him in—was broken by Mr. Bones. The vow was broken, and it didn't bother him.

He enjoyed seeing how happy people were at the event and taking pictures with him. Letting go of what used to matter was empowering, as he enjoyed what was directly in front of him. Mr. Bones didn't care if he had no literal influence on the surrounding party. To be front and center positively impacting the vibe of a three-day concert wasn't such a bad way to spend a weekend in his afterlife.

When it ended, he missed the stimulation, but welcomed what Buck had in mind. With the money made from online sales, events, and social media income, Buck didn't need to haul loads anymore. He transitioned to a full-time Mr. Bones entrepreneur. Keeping the purple truck for image and to haul event trailers became the new norm. They moved to the beach in southern Florida. Between events, Buck brought Mr. Bones to the beach and set up two lawn chairs to watch the waves. Wearing fun attire while lounging on the sand delighted existing fans and attracted new ones. Buck posted and streamed it all. People liked the beach Mr. Bones as much as the festival Mr. Bones. The #mrbones brand continued to grow, and seeing a Mr. Bones of different sizes on the front of more and more vehicles became a common phenomenon.

Buck had struck gold, and Mr. Bones enjoyed reclining on the beach and watching the world go by. The hundreds of girls in bikinis taking pictures with him on a regular basis didn't hurt, either. Of the different iterations of afterlife circumstances he had survived (for lack of a better word), Mr. Bones wondered if this would be the pinnacle of his afterlife? In all honesty, what could be better? Enjoying a similar standard of life in Buck's retirement and party lifestyle seemed as good as it could get. What is it to be dead if not officially retired from living?

Their next show was a #mrbones Christmas block party in New Orleans. The event showcased a Halloween on Christmas costume mashup with live DJs blasting their art for the crowds. Buck decorated Mr. Bones and his truck up with Christmas lights and donned an emo Santa Claus suit for the party. Mr. Bones went in the buff, save for a Santa hat, garland scarf, and tasteful string lights.

A feature of the show was to hold a costumed group picture contest with Mr. Bones to hail in the new year. The twelve best pictures voted for online would be professionally edited and compiled into a Mr. Bones 2024 calendar. The idea was a hit. Buck and Mr. Bones fans rallied to the occasion and took part wearing everything from scandalous to dramatic, comedic to professional, graceful to ridiculous. The overall result was a rockstar time had, another swell in the sale of merchandise, and countless more supporters for the #mrbones brand.

When the party was over, the odd duo returned to their south Florida retreat to count proceeds, plan the next event, and lounge on the beach to soak up the rays of stardom. Well, Buck did most of that. Mr. Bones just enjoyed the beach. More beach. More sun. More bikinis. More waves. Rockstar afterlife suited Mr. Bones. After the journey he'd had, it felt deserved. Like he'd earned it through his many trials.

With his former identity behind him and his vow broken, Mr. Bones wanted for nothing these days. Letting the good times roll felt as natural as it did when he was alive. Better yet, he had a manager! He didn't even have to do any of the work! Afterlife couldn't get any better than this.

***

Once upon a warm afternoon day five months into the new year, Buck and Mr. Bones lay reclining under a purple beach umbrella covered in rhinestones while dressed up in mariachi style sombreros with sugar skull face paint on. The former is sipping on a Cuba Libre with his open laptop on a wicker box he used as a table, brainstorming a 4th of July #mrbones show in Fort Lauderdale. The latter rested with his face painted, wearing his black and red sombrero, just sitting there as usual.

"Do you think planning the colors to be themed red, white, and black is too gimmicky? Do you think we should flare it up some, or stick with the classics that work?" Buck asked Mr. Bones. Mr. Bones stoically watched the sea. Two women in bikinis turned and waved at Buck as they walked by, noticing the bedazzled purple umbrella, no doubt. Or maybe it was the two big sombreros underneath it? "You do know best, Bones. Classics it is!" Buck declared. "Why change something that works? Okay, so we'll do the show in standard American colors omitting blue. Nobody really likes blue anyway, right? I think replacing it with black will give it some Halloween edge without being too busy. Four colors are definitely too busy."

Mr. Bones had to give Buck credit for where it was due. For such a negative first impression, the man knew how to work. He was constantly setting up the next gig and marketing for it relentlessly. They had a show just two weeks ago and here he was, planning another one a little more than a month away. The odd fellow had grown on Mr. Bones. Partly as a companion, but definitely as a business manager. It was clear that all by himself, Mr. Bones would not be a brand. That required living human diligence and—well—the ability to communicate with the living world.

After finishing up the adjustments on the colors for the merchandise concepts he was working on, Buck closed the laptop. Picking up his Cuba Libre, he took a noisy sip and watched the water. Polishing it off, Buck opened the cooler to the right of his beach chair and mixed another drink. He took a few loud *slurps,* burped, and set it down. Standing, Buck headed towards the water to cool off.

Watching him go, Mr. Bones thought about Buck's drink. He had never been a drinking man during his life, since it went against his moral principals back then. As a party-goer now, he wished he was alive enough to get into it. Buck and their fans sure made it look like fun at their shows.

Pondering what Buck's Cuba Libre tasted like, Mr. Bones watched Buck splash about in the waves in his rhinestone covered sombrero. He was pushing out a little farther from shore than chest deep. His bedazzled hat reflecting a thousand rays whenever he moved. Movement to the left caught Mr. Bones' attention. A handful of ladies in swimwear kicking around a soccer ball. Opting to watch the girls, Mr. Bones settled in to enjoy things he could see but not touch. Girls felt much like the Cuba Libre to him these days. He figured Buck got enough attention for the both of them, and he was happy for Buck. All the pictures and attention Mr. Bones did receive were more than most dead people got. Mr. Bones couldn't name any other dead celebrities that got their skull covered in lipstick from time to time.

Not so bad. Not so bad at all.

Focusing back on the sea, he glanced around the water for his companion. Puzzled, he looked harder for the big black and red sombrero that matched his own. He couldn't find it. As it turns out, Buck cooling off in the surf was the last time Mr. Bones would ever lay sockets on him. Buck never came back.

Part IV

Lost and Found

Chapter Twenty-Six

It was torture for him to watch regular happenings on the beach while he knew a man was drowning. Had drowned. Whichever the case, it didn't matter. Mr. Bones struggled against his inability to move, to yell, just like before. The living world realized there was something wrong long after the fact.

Buck was hauled from the water. Sirens, lights, and emergency vehicles swarmed the beach as the sun began to dip towards the horizon. After the ambulance, lifeguards, and passersby left the beach, Mr. Bones remained there beneath Buck's rhinestoned purple umbrella. Without a Buck, there was no Mr. Bones.

That echoed through his undead existence. Without a Buck—no Mr. Bones.

The implications were terrifying. What now?

Was he to wait until the tide came up and seized their chairs? Was he going into the ocean tonight? Oh, no. Not the ocean... Not into the world's blackest bathtub.

He didn't want to see the sprayers again, nor hear them laughing.

As the sun sank into the Atlantic, Mr. Bones witnessed in horror as the tide reached his beach chair. That ever constant ebb and flow of the surf gradually invaded his beachfront seat. The front legs of the chair started to give as the sand was washed away.

A feeling he hadn't felt in a very long time gripped him as the chair slowly sunk into the beach.

Panic.

His mind reeled as he waited for Buck to come grab him up. But Buck was gone. He'd watched him get gurneyed away after paramedics failed to revive him. Who would rescue him?

The chair legs shifted deeper into the churning wet.

Who *could* come for him? Nobody else even—

Sand giving way, Mr. Bones lurched forward, his sombrero shifting with movement and falling to the beach. A surge of surf came in, and his sombrero was washed out into darkness. He wasn't quite on the sand yet, but his bony feet met with the beach. Toes he couldn't feel disappeared into the wet. His panic blossomed into fright.

HELP! he wanted to yell. *HELP! Please! Anyone!*

But he knew there was no one there. The beach had been empty for hours. Mr. Bones was forgotten without Buck to make him relevant. No Buck, no Mr. Bones. Nobody had paid him any heed on the beach when they evacuated his manager. Nobody came for him. Beachgoers probably assumed Buck had some team or crew that would come retrieve his property. But Buck didn't. They were a two-man-team split asunder.

He was forgotten.

This would be the end.

His body would be washed out to sea and then, nothing. Nothing. He would never be found. How would anyone find him? He imagined himself being photographed on the seafloor by a diver. Inside of his own mind, he'd be screaming out at the fool scuba diver looking at him, but they wouldn't want to disturb his remains.

As the chair gave way, Mr. Bones fell to the churning sand. Buck's signature umbrella falling shortly thereafter. Hints of white swirls and the darkness of unilluminated grit engulfed his vision. This was it.

He would be washed out to sea, and that would be it. That would begin his nightmare of resting forever, in the dark, underwater.

Underwater.

Would he even be able to see? Probably not. It would likely be so dark that he'd never see light again. Although he wouldn't feel the pressure, he would know it was there. He'd know that when the ocean took him, he would never see colors again. Maybe he'd be consumed by something big enough, but he knew that was a joke. Nothing eats skeletons whole.

No. Separated piece by piece and scattered along the ocean floor in two-hundred pieces. The rumination made him wonder if he would be sentient in each part of his skeleton when it was apart. Would he see from his skull as well as his toes? The points of his spine and the end of his tail bone? Would he suddenly view reality like a two-hundred eyed insect in dozens of places within the ocean all at once?

It was a ridiculous thought, but one he didn't like. As he contemplated, he was dragged away from his parcel on the beach and began churning in the surf. The purple umbrella got snatched up quickly and took a quicker route into the deep. Suddenly, he heard faint voices, but he couldn't discern where from.

"Remy—Remy, grab it! C'mon, bro. Just get ahold of it!"

Was he hallucinating? Were these voices like Theo's and Judah's and Magda's and Jonas's and Pete's and Debra's back in the morgue? Like his formerly manifested caricatures of comfort?

"I got it, man. I got it! Get off my case, man. Dang!"

When Mr. Bones had been so gripped by worry that he ceased to think at all, he was yanked from the waves. At first, all he saw was further water. The churning and sloshing, ebbing and flowing. He hated it. Mr. Bones decided if he never saw water again, it would be too soon. The pressure washers were always too close in mind to enjoy anything wet ever again.

"I got the back, bro! You got the legs?"

"Yeah, man. I got the legs." Mr. Bones hadn't imagined the voices. Two men grabbed him from the surf. "Man, this was a stupid idea. What if they catch us, BJ?"

"Catch us doin' what?" BJ said. "Catch us keepin' this cash money from the ocean? You out of your dang mind, bro. Nobody wanted it, that's why they left it! Nah, this is going to be good, yo! Trust me."

"Well, what the heck do we do with it now?" Remy asked. "We got it. Now what?"

As the two ran up the beach, each holding one end of Mr. Bones in both hands, the other responded.

"Let's just get it to the truck. We'll figure out the next move later. First: we needa get outta here, bro. If anybody notices? We prolly screwed," BJ said.

Remy scoffed. "Dude, you know I'm on probation, man! Why do I do crap like this with you?"

BJ smiled. "Because you trust me. C'mon. Let's just get it outta here. Toss it in the back."

Without a count, the duo swung Mr. Bones back once and heaved him into the bed of a pickup truck, jump rope style. After crashing into the bed, Mr. Bones found himself staring up at the sky. It was primarily light-polluted from the city, but he could make out a few stars. He didn't really care who these two were. Seeing the sky was infinitely better than imagining the darkness of the sea.

The two men opened and closed doors to the truck before taking off. Mr. Bones wanted to thank God for being rescued from the depths, but opted to just watch the sky zip by instead.

Chapter Twenty-Seven

It was a rough ride, bouncing and tumbling about in the back of the pickup. Whichever young man was driving sure wasn't taking it easy on turns, nor the accelerator. Mr. Bones ricocheted from bulkhead to bulkhead, sliding amongst the miscellaneous trash littered around him in the truck bed. It reminded him yet again of the body farm. Of being in a wheelbarrow with other deceased and piled into a dumpster to await his turn on the business end of the pressure hose.

He isn't going to get chopped and sold out like a normal stiff. We're gonna have some fun with him instead.

Mr. Bones felt his panic rising. The truck bounced in and out of a pothole, sending plastic cups, a couple pieces of lumber, a spare tire, and an empty white and red cooler into the air. The scattered rubbish crashed all around him, but he wasn't seeing the garbage.

Gettem boss!

The sky had vanished for Mr. Bones. All he could see was the pulsing white water. His whole world was wet.

Waste'em.

He wished he could wake up from this bad dream. There was nothing he wanted more than for this to be a dream within a nightmare. Buck was gone. His newfound excitement dashed to nothing. If it wasn't for these rowdy, rubbish-hauling young men, he would have ended up in the ocean. In the depths, probably forever until his bones decomposed. Regardless of how triggering this entire experience is, at least they kept him from Davy Jones.

After arriving at their destination, BJ and Remy retrieved Mr. Bones and carried him up an outdoor staircase into an industrial looking building. It was dark inside the warehouse for several moments. The boys set him down on something and he heard them walk away.

A loud *pop* sounded through the space as lights flickered on throughout the warehouse. Mr. Bones sat on an old red couch with more than its fair share of stains. The room had artwork on the walls, along with posters of basketball players. Although the floor was rugged, it had several rugs with varying patterns and colors that didn't match, like they had been acquired by circumstance instead of purchased deliberately. A reasonably sized flat screen faced Mr. Bones from a modest TV stand across the room. This wasn't just a warehouse, this was a home.

BJ and Remy were talking in a neighboring room, but Mr. Bones couldn't make out what they were saying. He thought about Buck again, replaying the moment he set down his cursed Cuba Libre to take a quick dip. Mr. Bones found himself fighting the urge to be upset with Buck. How careless could he be? Everybody knows not to swim drunk. What was the matter with him? And now look at this situation. It's like Buck never considered what might become of Mr. Bones without his waddling, adventurous caretaker.

How selfish of him, Mr. Bones thought. But then it occurred to him how selfish *that* statement was as well. His friend had drowned only a matter of hours ago and he was criticizing him in death. What if Buck was like Raymond now? What if he was laying in a morgue somewhere, confused and outraged about not passing on from his body? When he thought of it that way, it was Mr. Bones who felt selfish.

When BJ and Remy returned to the room, they appeared in good spirits. BJ wore a purple hoody and baggy blue jeans with white high-tops. Remy was shorter than BJ and was wearing a Miami Dolphins tank top. He likewise had on baggy blue jeans and white sneakers. Remy plopped down in a brown recliner that likely survived the late 1980s from the looks of it. BJ sat next to Mr. Bones on the ragged red couch.

Picking up a TV remote from the riddled-with-nonsense coffee table in front of the sofa, BJ turned on the television and started flipping through channels.

"Yo, which news channel you think is most likely to cover the #mrbones dude drowning at the beach today?" BJ asked..

"Hm..." Remy contemplated. "When in doubt, I use WSFL! WSFL covers everything that's just grabby and kind of stupid. It's all headlines with them."

BJ grinned. "You right! Ol' WSFL." He continued flipping through channels. Looking back over at Remy, BJ said. "Uh, you remember which channel WSFL is on?"

"Channel 39."

"Right!" BJ exclaimed. "Man, I don't know how you remember all that kinda stuff. My mind hates numbers."

Remy wore an innocent grin and shrugged his shoulders. "I just see 'em, man. Oh, oh! That's it." Remy said, pointing at the screen. "Right there."

A female news anchor in a red blazer sat behind a desk on the TV. To her left on the screen was the picture of an attractive man sitting in a courtroom. Written below her in white block letters was the question:

ISRAEL STONE: SERIAL KILLER OR VICTIM?

The camera angle changed, and she turned to follow it. "Next up, Miami grieves the loss of one of its rags-to-riches locals that met with tragedy today on Miami Beach." Suddenly, a photo of Buck with Mr. Bones zip-tied to his big-rig appeared on screen.

BJ leaned forward in his seat, resting his elbows on his knees. "Bro, bro! This is it! Shh, shh!"

"You're the one talking, man," Remy replied.

BJ raised his hand up in mock seriousness to silence Remy. Rolling his eyes, Remy focused back on the TV.

"I think it's safe to say anyone with a smartphone watched the meteoric rise to stardom of Buck Tulley over the past couple of years and his skeletal partner in crime, Mr. Bones." The picture morphed from a still to a video of Buck dancing on stage at a festival underneath a banner that read #mrbones. "In a tragic turn of events, Mr. Tulley's body was retrieved from the water today after an unfortunate swim turned deadly."

Video of paramedics loading a shirtless Buck from a gurney into an ambulance replaced the cheery concert footage. "During Buck's final ride, he was pronounced dead on the way to the ER. To our knowledge, Buck left behind no family. Authorities are still attempting to track down if there was any plan in place to pass on Buck's lucrative #mrbones merchandise brand. Moreover," she paused as the video changed yet again to a still picture. Sitting on a red couch watching the news unfold before him, Mr. Bones recognized himself.

"Buck's beloved anatomical skeleton and namesake of his brand was left on the beach amidst the chaos of trying to rescue Buck. Authorities have returned to the beach in an attempt to collect the precious fan favorite. Thus far, Mr. Bones has not been found. The search will continue tomorrow, but authorities are afraid the prop may have been taken by the surf. More on that as updates come in. After a short break, Brandon has the weather. Thank you for watching WSFL News."

As the news network segued into a commercial break, BJ, his eyes wide and with a bit of a frown, looked at Remy. A boyish smile crept onto BJ's face. "So, what do you think we should do with our new friend here?"

Remy looked at their stolen cargo. "Well, we got away with it so far. They didn't mention a car or truck leaving the scene or anything. I think we grabbed it up and got out of their quick enough. But," Remy looked over at Mr. Bones, "how are we supposed to make money off of 'em? If we try to sell it, we could get caught."

"Caught doin' what, though?" BJ challenged. "What if we just say we foundem' and turn 'em in? We could say we saved it from going to the ocean. It's the truth anyway, ain't it?"

Remy scrunched up his eyebrows in thought. "That's all true enough, definitely. But they didn't say anything about a reward, right? I didn't hear nothin' about a reward. They don't even know if that Buck dude even has a business partner or anything to run his money and his stores and stuff. How would we get paid?"

As the boys discussed their predicament and Mr. Bones' future, Mr. Bones was busy watching the TV as the news came back on. The story being aired was not in Florida, but a national story about a church in Houston. A church he knew from his past life. Meadowview Megachurch was on the news once again. To Mr. Bones' continued displeasure, it wasn't receiving praise as it did while he lived. How long would his living legacy continue to haunt him when he wanted nothing more than to leave it behind?

Mr. Bones watched as they covered testimonies of women he recognized. They only showed snippets of three or four of them, but he instantly recognized all of them as women he had paid in exchange for growing the church, among other more intimate deeds. The final testimony came from than none other than Amanda Goode. Sitting in a beige blazer and matching skirt, she spoke about how she was putting the money she was awarded from Reverend Carter's vast estate to meaningful use. Amanda explained how she started a not-for-profit that focused on recovering from sexual abuse embedded in religious communities. The interviewer told her she was a hero and asked if she had a message for anyone out there actively suffering from sexual abuse. What would she say to them?

Amanda Goode looked at the camera and said, "I would tell them they are not alone. And to never give up. When it comes to facing your abuser, never let them buy you off. Hope for them to die and take their money instead."

The female interviewer chuckled at Amanda's words, and leaning forward, lightly touched her shoulder. "You are a model to young women everywhere, Amanda. You are so brave."

BJ and Remy hadn't even stopped their conversation to watch the interview. It was old news to them. They blocked it out as they discussed how to handle their newfound opportunity.

Chapter Twenty-Eight

"A'ight, I think we've brainstormed enough for tonight." BJ looked over at the immobile skeleton on his couch and pointed at it for emphasis. "We already got this thing, and the cops didn't seem to notice. So, I'd say we did good enough for now. I'm freakin' tired. And we still got that music video to work on tomorrow, remember?"

Remy let out an exasperated sigh. "Oh, dang. You right. We told the Holla Holla Boys we'd jam with them some and see if anything comes out good."

"Mhm. Yup. So, sleep now. We can deal with Bonesy here tomorrow. He ain't goin' anywhere," BJ said.

Realizing how tired he was as well, Remy laughed. "Naw, I don't think he'll be goin' anywhere, either. Alright, man. I'll catch you in the morning." Standing, Remy walked into a hallway, out of sight.

"A'ight, bro. Take it easy." BJ lifted the remote to turn off the TV, but hesitated. He looked over at their charge. "You prolly don't get to watch too much TV, huh Bonesy?"

Bonesy? Bonesy... Good grief. Don't these clowns KNOW who I am at this point? Mr. Bones. Mr.—Bloody—Bones.

"I'll leave it on for ya," BJ told him. "The noise usually helps me sleep, anyway. We'll discuss hocking you in the morning. Chill?" After waiting politely for a moment, BJ chuckled at his own wit. "Alright then, chill." Joking to himself, BJ turned off the light and walked out. Mr. Bones heard him open and close a door, and he was gone.

Mr. Bones sat idle while the TV painted him with colorful light. He didn't really enjoy being alone anymore. Now, thinking about it, he didn't think he ever enjoyed being alone. In life, he didn't talk to himself like many people do, because there was always someone around for him to communicate with. Whether a business related meeting or church group gathering, book signing, morality lecture, or entertaining a woman, there was always something to do.

Not anymore. Buck had really outdone himself to make Mr. Bones' afterlife the last year and a half profoundly exciting. It was terrible at first, no doubts there. He remembered when he first met Buck in Kelsey's yard. How much disdain he felt at Buck stealing him. How violated he felt.

The women he'd had relationships with in life felt violated as well, didn't they? So much so that they desired to pursue action after he passed. Like Buck, he hadn't thought about how his actions would make other people feel. Although he didn't like it, maybe his money being divided amongst those he hurt was justified?

And I'm dead, anyway. What else was my fortune supposed to accomplish?

He'd given himself a fantastic point. What else was his money supposed to do? Help those in need? Maybe those women *were* in need. Amanda was pursuing a different version of what he had been trying to do: help people.

Mr. Bones felt himself on a slippery slope inside of his own mind. How did he hurt people while trying to help them? Was it that easy to do? To slip into hurting individuals you are attempting to save?

After some pondering, he concluded it wasn't *Raymond Carter* who was supposed to be *saving* them. It was God. Raymond Carter should have been the conduit for the Lord to work through. Instead, Raymond acted as if he *was* God, didn't he? That's how he failed the women that he'd hurt. Whether or not he did it with intention was irrelevant. What's relevant is clear. They *were* hurt. They *are* hurt.

These intrusive ponderings left Mr. Bones feeling hollow. The news ended, and another program began. It was a documentary. Mr. Bones felt the title was all too fitting for his evening of self-reflection:

Reverend Raymond Carter: The Snake in the Garden

A series of video clips started playing a background of grim music. Some of them were snippets of his televangelist sermons. One was him volunteering at a women's shelter in Houston. Another was him at the pulpit in front of his stadium-sized congregation at Meadowview. A voice began speaking over the music while the videos continued to run.

"Who was Reverend Raymond Carter? Was he a priest or an entrepreneur? Was he a man of God or a man of himself? Was he a preacher—the music stopped dramatically, and the video turned to a still portrait of Raymond Carter—or a predator?"

Chapter Twenty-Nine

BJ and Remy bound through the door of the warehouse in an animated storm of enthusiasm. "BJ, yo that was *tight* what you spat today! Man, if you could keep it real like that *all* the time? Bruh—we would go viral for REAL!" Remy acted out a Michael Jackson hat tilt and spun on his heels like the King of Pop. He even stuck the ending, quickly transitioning to the toes of his shoes with his knees bent and feet together like MJ himself.

BJ smiled with all of his teeth. "Thanks, bro. And dude, if you could practice more moves like that? Rap videos or not, I think you could put a little somethin' somethin' together yourself. Help bring more draw to us and all." BJ turned his attention to Mr. Bones, still watching the news channel on the television. They hadn't turned the TV off when they left, nor moved Mr. Bones from his resting place on the dilapidated old couch.

Remy stood straight, beaming. "You really think so? It seems sorta out of place in a rap video. Should I actually work on some dancing? You think that could bring all the girls to the yard?"

The last comment had BJ spitting out a laugh. "Bro, you work on anything enough, and uh—YEAH—it can bring the girls to the yard!" They both laughed and slapped hands. "Am I right?" BJ said with sass.

"You usually are, man. You usually are." Remy focused on Mr. Bones then, as well. "Alright, speaking of viral, let's get to Phase 2 of today's agenda." Walking across the room, Remy took his seat next to Mr. Bones like the night before. BJ sat and leaned back in his vintage recliner.

"So, we are trying to get attention to turn this dude in—" he said, indicating Mr. Bones. "—and claim a reward, without looking like we stole 'em, right?"

"Right." Remy echoed.

"I say we go with what we brainstormed on the way to the jam today. I think we make a brand new Instagram with a brand new email—so folks don't know it's us—and do some anonymous posts with Bonesy here and his hashtag. Maybe whoever worked with that Buck dude will contact us about a reward for finding their property."

Remy thought it over, drawing his thumb and forefinger down both sides of his jaw. "I mean, I like it. It's straightforward, but still keeps us in the background so we won't get in trouble. They either notice and give us a reward, or don't notice and we stay safe. It ain't like they've put a number on the news for us to call or anything to turn 'em in."

"Mhm," BJ said. "Thus far, the news is being how it usually is. Totally freakin' useless. They did that one story on Buck and Bonesy yesterday and that's it. I haven't seen another one yet."

"Dang..." Remy lamented. After a brief pause, he added, "Okay. Let's get the Instagram going then and set up our first post." Leaning back dramatically, Remy spread his arms out in front of himself and looked into the space like he was imagining something grand. "I'm picturing us dressed up like we're doing a music video, except we do the gangster look, and put some sort of masks on so people don't see our faces. We set it up all cool lookin', pose with our homie here, and send a message that we gottem' and we are chill with a reward to return 'em."

"I'm into where your head's at," BJ said. "What do you wanna call the Instagram?"

Remy raised an eyebrow as he pursed his lips in a half-silly, half serious expression. His eyes lit up with an idea. He typed a message in his phone, then turned it around to show BJ.

Screwing up his face in disgust, BJ shot Remy a glare. "Bruh, ew, no. That ain't no good at all."

Remy looked deflated. "Why not?"

Tilting his chin down, BJ looked like the older brother Remy didn't have. "We got bones? C'mon, bro! That makes us sound horny or desperate. Just plain weird. You gotta think about junk like that when you're trying to market something."

Drawing into himself a little, his shoulders slumping, Remy looked sheepishly back at BJ. "Oh, well, when you put it like that... I see it now."

"Mhm," taunted BJ. "I bet you do." BJ mumbled under his breath, "My dude over here callin' us the brothers with the boners. Pfft. Shaking my dang head."

"Okay," Remy interjected. "What would *you* call it, then?"

BJ looked at Mr. Bones for a moment, then answered. "I was thinking something simple and to the point. Like, Mr. Bones Reward or, Attention Mr. Bones Brand. I don't know! I just want the message out there and obvious so we can turn it in, get some cash, then invest it in our album—

"What about Lost and Found?" Remy interrupted.

Looking at him, BJ grinned. "Bro, if that isn't already a taken handle? I'm into it. Check it! Check it!"

Remy was already typing. A smirk split his right cheek. "It's available like this:"

@lost_n_fownd

He handed the phone over to BJ. Looking at it, BJ nodded his head. "I like it. To the point, still got a little artistic marketing in it. Fo sho, bro." He extended his fist, Remy bumped it. "Alright, let's get dressed up—like not exactly what we wore to jam today—and then we decide where to take the photo and how to pose Bonesy."

Remy had an idea. "Should we dress Mr. Bones up, too? I mean, he is a prop, after all."

BJ's toothy grin reappeared. "I like where your head is at. Sure. Let's pick out an outfit for boney-homie, too." BJ stood and looked down at Mr. Bones, still sitting on the couch. "You gonna be stylin' like you've never styled before, my dude."

Chapter Thirty

Waiting until the golden hour when the sun has barely touched the horizon, and the beautiful last shudder of day bathes everything in brilliant light, BJ and Remy set up outside the warehouse for their first post. On a patio on the west side of the building, they had some of the basic staples for weight lifting. A simple bench press, one pullup bar they built themselves, and an ancient pulley machine with a few attachments they picked up from a garage sale. It wasn't much, but it was enough to keep them ripped for their rap videos. The guys wore Lakers' colors and dressed Mr. Bones up in fake gold chains. The fitness-themed photo was snapped and posted under the new social media handle @lost_n_fownd.

Over the next several days, BJ and Remy did similar photoshoots all around the warehouse. Each time they took the pictures at golden hour and each photo had its own flare. An industrial-themed photo resulted in a comic, yet macabre, snap of Mr. Bones dangling by a hook on the end of a steel cable above the two men. They were wearing blue coveralls and white undershirts, their arms crossed with a mask of seriousness covering their jovial nature.

BJ's idea for a photo op featured a rental car and a hired checkout girl who worked in a nearby shopping mall. Remy thought it was a foolish waste of funds, but BJ was of the mindset you need to spend money to make money. For only about a hundred dollars, BJ rented a super red 2022 Chevy Corvette Stingray to pose with. Thanks to Erica from Bath and Bodyworks in a black bikini and some Monopoly money, Mr. Bones and the boys had their final Instagram picture. Mr. Bones got to relive an old glory moment during the last shoot that reminded him of Buck. Erica had him in her lap on the hood of the Corvette, kissing him on his bony cheek.

***

One week passed since BJ and Remy launched their new Instagram @lost_n_fownd, and although the posts were bringing in followers due to #mrbones, there hadn't been one titter about offering a reward. As excited as they were about the posts gaining traction and praise for the quality of the pictures, no actual money was in sight.

On a more positive note, there was no talk of police or crime committed either. It seemed no one really cared if Buck's skeletal prop was found, washed out to sea, or long-term borrowed by an obsessed fan. A few days after the first week of posts and waiting, the news finally covered something pertinent to BJ and Remy.

BJ was in the kitchen making popcorn and grilled cheese with pickles for them while Remy was waiting for the news. When the story came on, Remy went ballistic.

"BJ! BJ, it's on, man. Get in here!"

From the kitchen, BJ. "Okay, okay! Gimme like, 2 minutes, bro! I gotta make sure not to burn lunch."

"All good. I'm honed in. I won't miss nothin'" Remy said. The jingle rang for WSFL News while the logo rotated and settled onto the center of the screen. Wearing a blue jumpsuit today, the female anchor sat in the station with a picture of Buck and Mr. Bones on the top left of the screen. She introduced the story.

"The nation has been beside itself with curiosity regarding the death of social media entrepreneur Buck Tulley since his tragic demise almost two weeks ago. Our reports tell us that his untimely passing has spiked sales on his popular internet brand #mrbones. Despite his absence and the Mr. Bones tour coming to a premature halt, fans far and wide are sporting their #mrbones merchandise all across the nation."

Rushing in with a plate piled high with pickle grilled cheeses and a hefty bowl of butter popcorn, BJ set the food on the coffee table with purpose, then took his seat on the tired red couch next to Mr. Bones and Remy. Remy grabbed a grilled cheese while BJ started a steady mechanical chomping of popcorn, bowl to mouth.

"Well, the question we've all been waiting for has finally been answered. George is over in Nashville, Tennessee with the breaking news." She smiled at the camera as the feed switched to another place. A brick and white trim mansion came into view. A Georgian-style town house that looked to have more than a dozen rooms sat on a beautifully landscaped plot of land.

The shot zoomed in as the feed switched to a study inside the mansion. Two people sat at a circular oak table between two marble busts. A man wearing a black blazer was laughing with a woman much older than him wearing an ivory-colored pantsuit. As the laughing came to a close, the anchor began talking.

"I'm George Johnson coming to you live from here in Nashville, Tennessee. Sitting with me here today is someone that surprised us at the station yesterday with a simple phone call. Meet Mrs. Marjorie Bell. How are you doing this sunny afternoon in Nashville?"

Marjorie Bell had noticeable blue eyes that likely shined brighter in her youth. Her eyes contrasted sharply with the white curls that appeared around the brim of her ivory rim hat decorated with black lace. She smiled as she started speaking.

"Hello, Mr. Johnson. I'm doing well. Thank you for asking." Her voice had a southern air of command in it, like she has been making demands of people for a long time. If she didn't look like a grandmother, the pretentiousness would be distasteful. "Although I know why you are here, do your viewers a kindness by explaining to them why your news crew stands in my home today." Marjorie said it with a smile, but George looked a little anxious before turning red and chuckling off the awkwardness of the suggestion.

"Of course, ma'am! Of course. So—let's get right into it. All of us at WSFL News have been boggled the past week regarding Mr. Buck Tulley and his successful internet brand, #mrbones. With him leaving behind no will and possessing no form of partner or corporation, it has been the topic of much interest what will happen to the continued revenue and ownership of the brand. As we've been informed here at WSFL News, you are a relative of Buck Tulley. Is that true, Mrs. Bell?"

The black plume sticking out of a bed of dark lace in her hat danced as she nodded her head with practiced grace. "Why, yes, Mr. Johnson. That is true. Buck Tulley is my embarrassing nephew. We didn't talk much, not unless Buck wanted something. Usually money. My brother and I, Buck's father, grew apart many years ago. We hadn't talked in, oh, almost twenty years when he died about a decade ago. The last time I saw Buck, I helped him buy that god awful eighteen-wheeler some years back so he could become a truck driver. To his credit, he did pay the money back. He wasn't a bad man, my nephew, but I wouldn't say I was proud to call him my relative, Mr. Johnson."

George Johnson raised his eyebrows and looked at the camera with a big smile. "Wow. Your nephew. Small world! Isn't it, Mrs. Bell?"

Marjorie Bell looked at him the way a grown cat looked at a kitten. "Sometimes Mr. Johnson, yes. It sure can be."

BJ reached for and stacked two grilled cheeses on top of each other and started eating. With half the popcorn gone, Remy opted to bring the bowl to his lap and began shoveling mouthfuls while they watched.

George Johnson chuckled off the silence before continuing. "Well, that would make *you* his only known next of kin, Mrs. Bell. You are aware of how profitable the #mrbones brand has become in the past year and a half, aren't you? Your nephew was working with festivals, running merchandise tours, getting paid photo operations, and even modeling with his skeletal companion towards the end. He has made quite a name for himself online, and his brand continues to soar after his recent passing. By the way, Mrs. Bell, I am so sorry for your loss."

Marjorie Bell smoothed a few wrinkles out of her ivory sleeves. After getting comfortable again, she reengaged George Johnson. "I have been made aware of his recent merits. I must say that although I am impressed, I personally don't want to involve myself with his brand or what he was working on at the time of his death. I have decided to donate his semi-truck to a collector that has contacted me with an interest in it. After that? I intend to wash my hands of it. Rest in peace, nephew."

A million-dollar smile spread across George Johnson's face. "Well, thank you for enlightening us about some of the questions people have been asking. Mrs. Bell, can I ask you one more question on the matter before we take a break?"

"Sure. One more question." She smiled prettily at the camera, blinking like she had just won prom queen.

Glancing at the camera before talking, George responded. "Alright then! The situation regarding Buck Tulley's skeleton prop, the namesake of the #mrbones brand, went missing on the beach the day that he drowned. It has been trending online if there is to be a reward for the return of the prop. What is your thoughts on that?"

Marjorie scoffed. "My thoughts on that are I don't care about one of his props. He has them for sale through his store online and they are replaced easily. I don't see anything special regarding the one left on the beach. So, no. I do not intend to issue any reward for the return of his prop. With so many hundreds or thousands of them strapped to the front of cars I see everywhere these days, it would likely be a fake, anyway."

BJ lost his grilled cheese halfway between bites as it fell to the floor. Remy choked on a handful of popcorn. Mr. Bones rested motionless, because he's dead and can't move.

"Alright, folks. There you have it! George Johnson at WSFL News bringing you this interview live with answers to your trending online inquiries. If there is nothing else you would like to say, Mrs. Bell, I think that concludes our talk today."

Marjorie Bell smiled. "I think I've had enough talk today. Thank you, George Johnson."

It was all George could do to not roll his eyes at the woman. Laughing it off, he said, "Okay! Well, thank you so much for sharing your time with us today, Mrs. Bell. I hope you have a wonderful afternoon. Back to you, Sharyl."

When the feed switched back to the WSFL station, BJ reached for the remote and turned off the TV. They sat in silence a moment before Remy broke it.

"What should we do now, BJ?" He sounded a bit defeated. Forlorn. They'd spent more than a week on this project and were both excited to invest funds into their music.

BJ screwed up his face and looked over at Remy. "I don't know, bro. I guess we've just—got him now."

Remy sighed as he unlocked his phone. "Well, at least Insta likes our new handle and the posts with the Mr. Bones hashtag."

"Yeah," was all that BJ could manage.

"We might as well just keep doing photo shoots with him then, right? It can't hurt. Maybe we should feature some music videos with him, since people like the photo posts," Remy suggested.

"Yeah, why not," BJ said. "Ain't like he's worth anything after that interview."

Chapter Thirty-One

Mr. Bones spent the past ten days or so with BJ and Remy in a sort of dormant state, for lack of a better word. After watching the aftermath of Reverend Carter's death on the news, followed by that documentary made about his life and legacy, he was feeling quite numb. He wasn't really sure how he was supposed to feel. The reality is, he couldn't interact with his new owners, anyway. What was the point in being present while they hatched their plan to turn him in for cash?

Furthermore, why bother having any feeling either way regarding their photo shoots and Instagram antics and all the other plans they had been working on? He couldn't stop them, nor help them. Not to offer his opinion, enthusiasm, or outrage at one of their efforts. They didn't even know he was in here, trapped as he was. Stuck. Wedged within his own bones. Mentally, emotionally, and spiritually decaying as a dead immortal soul.

Someone looking from the outside at Mr. Bones' predicament might expect more from his attitude. Have some faith, one of his former flock might suggest. Could this be one long, long, *long* trial of which a finish line existed? Or is his current perspective more reflective of the truth? This is it.

This is all there ever was, and all that will ever be. Enjoy the ride while it is in front of you, whatever that ride may be. Because one day, it will all change before your eyes and be born anew. And it is entirely possible that, as in most cases, that change won't be what you would have desired. Blissful reality is as wonderful as it is finite.

For the time being, he neither objected nor triumphed; prayed or cursed; lamented or fought. For now, he simply existed without expectation or intentional feeling of any kind. The only desire left in the hollows of his decomposed material form was to observe what was to come. Nothing more, nothing less. Merely observe, like plankton, drifting on currents beyond his control. Within that acceptance, he searched for peace.

***

One afternoon, Remy received an odd message on the @lost-n-fownd account. After telling BJ about it, the duo had a decision to make.

Although there is no formal reward for the return of Mr. Bones to Buck's brand, someone is offering to buy the prop from them. The Instagram handle seemed normal enough. It looked like this:

@et_tu_brute93

Originally skeptical, BJ looked over Remy's shoulder as he investigated the account.

It only had 86 followers, but followed 316. Most of the 19 posts made on the account were of food, desert scenery, and some super weird art from a gallery neither man recognized. The bio read:

Art Enthusiast — New Collector

"Could it be a scam?" Remy asked.

BJ, pacing, responded. "I mean, anything *could* be a scam. But it isn't even that much money, is it? How much did you say they are offering?"

"$1,500," Remy said.

"$1,500," BJ echoed. He was ringing his hands together, his tongue stuck out to wet his lips. "It isn't a ton of money, but that's a lot of dough to put into our music. I don't know. Bonesy is cool and all, but we were always just going to turn him in for a reward anyway, right? Wasn't that the whole idea?"

Remy screwed up his face into a considerate frown. He looked over at the skeleton they had propped up in the corner. "Our followers think it's a cool addition to our photos. It got that Buck guy famous and made him a boat-load of money," Remy said half to himself.

Ceasing the pacing, BJ turned to face him. "That guy was touring all over the country with this thing on his grill. That's an entirely different thing than what we have going on here! You really think adding this silly thing to our videos and photo shoots is going to somehow transform us into billionaires?"

Remy didn't respond. He remained in thought, looking at the message with the anonymous buyer on his phone.

"Whereas this—" BJ walked over to where Remy sat on the couch, pointing down at his phone—"*this* is actual cash that some nerd wants because they were probably a fan of Buck when they were touring. Heck, they're probably into the festival scene and know Bonesy from one of the shows. Regardless, I like the idea of money right now in our hands, which is why we took the thing from the beach in the first place."

Remy was shaking his head slowly. "I'm just thinking about brand-ing and everything. The hashtag definitely helped us online to get people paying attention to our posts. What if we stuck with it for a while?"

Slamming his hands into his pockets, BJ went back to pacing. Stopping again, he turned. "Remy."

Remy looked up at his best friend from his phone.

"Money we could have now is better than hoping it comes later," BJ said. "New gear, maybe some advertising, some travel money. Maybe we could go on tour. Shoot some music. Make more content. We could probably do that with fifteen-hundred bucks. It ain't like we could quit our jobs yet or anything—but it's a start." He started pacing again. Then excitedly, stopped and shot his hand out towards Remy. "It's a big drop into our bucket, Remy!"

An exasperated sigh escaped Remy's mouth. "If this is really what you wanna do, I'm in. It was your idea to take it from the beach in the first place."

BJ leapt into the air. "That's what I'm talkin' about, Remy!" Settling down, BJ smoothed his t-shirt, like it got wrinkled during his excitement. "Ask them when and where they want to meet. Let's organize this thing." He looked over at Mr. Bones sitting in the corner. "Sorry, Bonesy old pal. Business is business. No hard feelings."

As Remy typed a response to the potential buyer, BJ stepped out of the room and into the kitchen. Mr. Bones thought nothing. The numbness continued as he consciously tried to meditate more often than not.

Let one moment bleed into the next. May my existence transform into a peaceful blur. Perchance someday, I will sleep forever.

Chapter Thirty-Two

@lost_n_fownd: so where you at?

@et_tu_brute93: head south on ocean drive. when you see the trees, turn left on inlet boulevard. drive until you see a parking lot. park there. then walk to the south pointe cafe. come after the cafe closes, after it's dark. I'll meet you there.

South Pointe Cafe is near the South Pointe Hills, near Miami Beach. It is the southernmost region of the island where the famous stretch of beach resides on its eastern coast. The boys didn't like the ominous tone of the message, but they understood. Both of them had purchased or sold dodgy products from dodgy parties in the past. Even though this wasn't necessarily an illegal transaction, it was admittedly sketchy.

Technically, they stole Mr. Bones from the beach. BJ and Remy were well aware of that. The worry that this was a sting operation crossed their minds more than once, but nothing on the news or Internet led them to believe the police were after Buck's missing prop at all. It seemed like authorities didn't rightly care, since Buck Tulley's next of kin appeared on television without pressing charges or causing a fuss regarding the missing property. After all, BJ and Remy initially posted that they had the missing property almost two weeks ago. @et_tu_brute93 was the first person to take any interest in Mr. Bones, the actual prop, whatsoever.

BJ's pickup just made the left onto Inlet Boulevard and into the wooded area. It was uncomfortably dark in the surrounding trees. They left the street lights of Miami ten minutes ago on Ocean Drive before reaching South Pointe. Remy looked around from the passenger seat with unease. BJ put on his bravest face, acting like everything was under control.

"I really don't like this," Remy admitted.

"I feel ya," BJ said. "It's chill though. Ain't nobody going to kill us or something over a silly Internet dummy. This dude is probably just—freakin' weird, you know? The kinda dude that hits people up online to buy a realistic skeleton off of Instagram. It's already a strange thing to do. Meeting after dark at some closed cafe isn't that far off from that."

Remy peered out the window, hoping to spot the parking lot soon. "I guess, man. I admit, I don't get why someone would hurt us over it. It just gives me the creeps. That's all. I'm no gangbanger. Never have been. I *am* on probation for that drug thing, though. I'm just hoping to make money creating music with my best dude while staying outta jail. Nothing more."

BJ looked over at him. "It'll be fine, bro. Promise. It's all good." He offered his fist. Remy rolled his eyes, but ultimately bumped the fist.

"Yo, I think that's it," Remy said. Ahead of them was a parking lot with no lighting. There were no other vehicles parked there. Just a dumpster and an outhouse on the far side.

BJ pulled into and parked in a spot on the right side. The headlights of his truck illuminating a wooden fence. Beyond the fence was a long walkway that led to a large circle. Next to the walkway was a sign that read South Pointe Cafe. "Alright, bro. I think we're here," BJ said.

"Ugh. Okay, man. Let's just—let's just get this over with. I better not get robbed," Remy said.

"You ain't got no money anyhow," BJ mocked. "What they gonna take?"

"What about your truck?"

BJ looked at Remy in legitimate shock. "Don't even play like that, bro," he said, unbuckling his seatbelt. Opening the door, he climbed out. "Don't even play like that. That ain't even funny." He shut the door and walked to the rear of the truck.

"I wasn't playing," Remy said to himself before stepping out of the truck.

BJ jumped into the bed and picked up Mr. Bones, then handed him down to Remy. Grabbing the skeleton a bit awkwardly, Remy fussed with the dangling arms and one of the legs, nearly falling down. Laughing as he jumped down from the bed, BJ helped to steady his friend.

"You sure you got him, bro?" BJ's smile cut the darkness somewhat. Remy didn't chuckle.

"Come on. Let's just go meet this person and hope for the best." BJ tried holding onto one of Mr. Bones' bouncing arms as Remy held him haphazardly.

"Man, just let it go!" Remy insisted, hiking Mr. Bones higher onto his shoulder. "I got it now. Just walk in front of me. Make sure I don't trip over anything."

Still recovering from laughing, BJ conceded. "Alright, alright, bro. Will do." He took the lead, and the duo made their way down the long concrete path.

Mr. Bones watched the darkness bounce along as his head tossed and turned on Remy's shoulder. It seemed he would be changing hands yet again. So be it. He didn't dislike BJ and Remy, but he didn't particularly like them either. Getting attached to people when you're a non-living commodity is unhealthy. Mr. Bones embraced his inability to control what happened to him. The Carrie Underwood song *Jesus, Take the Wheel* came to mind. Except in this circumstance, there is no Jesus and there is no wheel. Along yet another path, he traveled, unable to choose his direction.

The three souls arrived at a circular concrete expanse. BJ took out his phone and shined his light around. Dark green bushes and trees encircled the place. Ahead of them, BJ and Remy could see chairs stacked atop outdoor tables in front of what must be the South Pointe Cafe. The circle they stood in was painted a bright blue that matched the decorative trim of the cafe. Utilizing his flashlight, BJ continued to search around the open space. No one was in sight.

"Yo, Remy. Maybe I should take Bonesy and you should text the dude and see what's up."

"Nah, man," Remy protested. "I'm already situated. Here, get up in my pocket and text him for me. You know my password."

BJ recoiled in exaggerated disgust. "You know I ain't trying to dig up in your pocket!"

"Shh!" Remy scolded. "Dude, for real. Quit being dramatic. Just—get in my pocket, and text the dude."

"Pfft," BJ scoffed. "Whatever. Best not say nothin' to anyone about it." BJ retrieved the phone and unlocked it.

@lost_n_fownd: we are here.

@et_tu_brute93: hang tight.

"What's he saying?" Remy asked.

BJ kept staring at the phone, hoping for more. "Told us to hang tight."

Shrugging his shoulders like a chill shuddered through him, Remy adjusted Mr. Bones. He scanned the eerie gloom pushing in on them. The sound of crashing waves in the distance persisted through the darkness. Headlights rounded a corner onto Inlet Boulevard. BJ and Remy turned to watch as a van of indiscernible color crawled towards the parking lot. They exchanged glances as it parks on the opposite side from BJ's pickup. The driver, passenger, and sliding door of the van opened and multiple people climbed out.

"Dang it, man," Remy said, trepidation in his voice. "Man, I don't like that." He looked over at BJ. "I don't like the look of *that* at all, man."

"Just be cool," BJ encouraged. His chest puffed out, making himself look thicker than he actually was. Even if he didn't admit it, Remy could tell he was on high alert.

The group from the van spread out, taking different routes towards them. A few cut through the grass while a big one walked confidently down the paved path. They were surrounding the boys. BJ was trying to count how many there were. He thought there were four. Two on each side. Watching the fifth approach, he realized the man was huge. Probably a foot taller than his six-foot-one frame.

Alongside the perimeter of the circle, the four stopped a good distance from each other. They wore dark hooded sweatshirts with the hoods pulled up. Neither BJ nor Remy could make out any of their faces. As the big one kept approaching, the duo pressed their shoulders together, almost back to back. Feeling this may have been a mistake, the duo prepared for a fight. Mr. Bones was meditating, almost mentally unresponsive to the action unfolding around him.

The giant stopped in front of them. He also wore a dark hooded shirt. All that could be seen was his big white chin, shining defiantly in the darkness.

"Hello," he said. The voice was deep, nasal. Heavily accented. It sounded almost Russian. Looking around the clearing, he focused back on BJ and Remy. "Nice night, no?"

Remy looked at BJ, then shouldered him. BJ gave him an up and down look, then stepped forward towards the big man. He stayed outside of arm's reach, but didn't want to appear intimidated. "So, my partner has Mr. Bones. Where's the money?"

The big man smiled beneath his hood. "Money? You stole it. Why should I give you any money?"

BJ shifted his weight. His heart racing as adrenaline dumped into his system. "We agreed on a price. I'm just asking that you honor it. We don't need any trouble here." Remy looked around at the surrounding goons. None moved. They just stood there, maddeningly still. He noticed how short they were compared to this guy. But it didn't matter how many there were. He and BJ were severely outnumbered.

"I'd like to propose a new deal," the accented giant said. BJ cursed under his breath. "I suggest you hand over Mr. Bones, and we won't take it from you."

BJ turned to see Remy. Remy's eyes pleaded with him. *Just let them have it,* they said. *It isn't worth it.* BJ faced down the brute. "This is *messed* up, bro! We're just trying to make a living out here!" His anger was getting the better of him. "We agreed on fifteen-hundred dollars. I want my fifteen-hundred dollars!"

BJ's heartbeat was in his ears. He was starting to have trouble thinking. His fists balled tightly without even realizing it. Was this a fight he could win?

The big man stepped slowly around BJ and towards Remy. BJ reared back, but didn't let the punch loose. It didn't phase the hooded figure. The giant extended a hand out towards Remy. "Please? Make this easy on everyone. Hand me the skeleton."

Remy looked at BJ. BJ was still half-cocked, his nerve slipping. BJ glanced at Remy for direction. Remy looked terrified. With shaking hands, Remy slowly lowered Mr. Bones from his shoulder and handed him to the hooded man.

"Remy!" BJ shouted in a whisper, lowering his fist. "What are you doin', bro?"

"I'm handling this," Remy snapped at BJ. Looking back at the big accented guy extending his hand, Remy handed over Mr. Bones.

The giant took the skeleton with one hand and draped it over his colossal shoulder. Looking up, he glanced around at his hooded comrades. As if planned ahead of time, one of them jogged up to the over-sized thief.

Giving BJ and Remy a wide berth, the smaller hooded figure reached out and seized one of Mr. Bones' feet, raising a flashlight. Switching it off, it nodded to the big guy and ran back to where they'd stood.

Satisfied, the big man reached into his pocket and handed something to BJ.

Triggered but confused, BJ snatched the bill from his hand. It was a $100 bill.

"So, we're gonna be wanting about fourteen more of these," BJ said, but the hooded man had already turned and started walking back towards the parking lot.

"This is messed up!" BJ called after him. "You know this is messed up!"

Remy stepped closer to BJ. "Let it go, BJ. Just let it go. It's whatever."

BJ's chest heaved. He already had plans for the fifteen-hundred. He looked down at the measly hundred dollars. "Dude," Remy said. BJ looked at his best friend. "We took it; it got taken from us. Let it go."

Nodding, BJ heard him.

The four surrounding them turned and jogged towards their leader. Piling into the van, the five loaded up, the engine turned over, and they drove off into the night.

Chapter Thirty-Three

On a different road, once again. The stranger put Mr. Bones in the back seat of the van and buckled him up. He had to admit; it was nice not just being tossed into the bed of a trash-filled truck. BJ and Remy weren't exactly gentle with him. It isn't that he felt any pain. Of course not, but it was the principle of the action. Why would anyone enjoy feeling like cargo bouncing around with rubbish? The cloaked giant treated him with care, gingerly placing him in one of the backseats like he was an old friend. The seatbelt was a true surprise. They treated him like he could die again. Sure, pointless, but good in principle.

As the van bumped down the road, the mood is—off. Mr. Bones couldn't quite put his bony finger on what, but something was. The big man that took him from Remy and tucked him in so gently was sitting in the passenger seat. Two more sat behind him, snickering. Snickering? These were thugs. They just robbed BJ and Remy. And they were snickering? That did seem off.

No one had yet said a word. The figure next to him turned quickly to look out the window. No doubt watching to see if BJ and Remy would give chase. They must have been satisfied with what they found, because the figure turned back and moved forward in their seat.

"Krumlov, you were amazing! Oh, my God! I was convinced you were as terrifying as you were supposed to be!"

It was a feminine voice. So all of his kidnappers weren't men.

A voice from the back spoke up. "Yeah, Krumlov. You nailed it, dude. I had no idea you could be so intimidating!" It was a man's voice—a young man. It wasn't deep and harrowing like the man in the front seat.

The van turned a corner and headed for the street lights of the city. As it did, the driver turned and addressed the girl sitting next to Mr. Bones. "Does this mean we can take our hoods down now?" The driver said. Also, a female voice.

"Like, seriously?" Came another feminine voice from the back seat.

"Yup. I think it's safe to say we are in the clear. It worked!" The woman next to him said, taking down her hood.

"Finally," said the male from the back seat. "It's way too flippin' warm to be dressed like this, even at night around here."

Mr. Bones remained confused. Some of these voices seemed familiar. Why did they seem so familiar? He searched his recent memory. Maybe from one of Buck's festivals?

The van passed beneath a streetlight, casting a quick line of illumination throughout the interior. For a moment, he saw the person next to him. Black hair. Pale complexion. She was sitting forward in her seat, still chatting with the big man in the passenger seat.

"Are you alright, Krumlov? I was worried that guy was going to hit you for a minute! Scared the crap out of me," she said.

The giant turned back towards her while he lowered his hood. "It was fine. I've been hit before. Isn't so bad." That deep, thick Russian sounding accent seemed to vibrate the upholstery. "It would have been fine."

"Well," she continued, "I'm glad I didn't have to see it. Good job. Good job, everyone!" She looked around the van, addressing each person. "Coco," she said to the driver. Turning around, she addressed those in the back. "Travis, Ariana, you guys all did *great*! That couldn't have gone any better!"

Travis? Ariana? No...

It can't be.

Someone leaned forward from the back seat. The van passed under another streetlight. "A solid plan from our fearless leader. Way to go, Kelsey. You got him back. Finally!"

Kelsey?

"Took you long enough," Ariana said from the back seat. "It's all you could talk about for what?" The question hung in the air. "A year? How long has she rambled on about this silly thing?"

"Certainly the whole time I've known her," Coco said. Another feminine voice. Higher pitched and squeakier than the other two women. "And we met before senior year, so, yeah. It's been quite a while."

"I'm glad you got him back, Kelsey," Krumlov rumbled. "I'm glad I could help with the—how do you say—scary part."

Everyone laughed. Mr. Bones remained in shock. The girl next to him shifted, so she was almost facing him as they sat side by side. When another streetlight whizzed by, he saw her. Her dark hair had grown since he saw her last. It was much longer. She still kept it in twin braids. The heavy makeup was gone, replaced with more complimentary tones. Much lighter. Her smile melted what was left of his heart, long decayed from his body.

"I never stopped looking for you," Kelsey said. "I'm sorry it took me so long. I had to graduate from high school." She smirked. "It took longer than I wanted, *trust* me."

Mr. Bones sat flabbergasted. His mind hadn't yet caught up with reality. Could it really be her? After all of this time?

"We'll have plenty of time to catch up," Kelsey said. "For now, we need to get on the road! We're a long way from home out here in—gross—Miami."

"Hey, I don't think it looks that bad!" Coco said, turning away from the road for a second to announce. "It looks like it could be fun!"

"Yeah, right," Ariana said from the back seat. "Fun if you're into thong bikinis and alligators."

"I like thong bikinis and alligators," Travis added.

"Nobody cares, Travis!" all three girls said in unison. Krumlov and Travis both laughed.

"Okay, so—van vote," Kelsey said. "All in favor of getting to the festival? If we leave tomorrow, we can probably get there in a few days."

The other four raised their hands and shouted, "Aye!"

"Cool. Alright," Kelsey said. "Let's get to camp and we'll set up for the night. Push on tomorrow." The van was silent for a few minutes. Just the sound of tires on pavement and the passing by of Miami traffic could be heard as they entered downtown. "Hey guys?" she said, addressing the whole van.

"What's up?"

"Yeah?"

"Hmm?"

She cleared her throat. "I just wanted to thank all of you for coming out here and doing this with me. You didn't have to, and it means so much to me. I couldn't have done it alone for so many reasons. From the bottom of my heart," Kelsey's voice cracked under the sudden rise of emotion. "Thanks for helping me get my skeleton—Amicus—back after he was stolen from me."

Krumlov turned and placed a hand on top of hers, resting on her knee. Travis and Ariana leaned forward, offering a hand on either shoulder. Coco looked in the rearview mirror and met Kelsey's wet eyes.

"We'd follow you anywhere, Kelse." Coco said. "Plus, who turns down a cross country adventure to steal back something meaningful that was stolen when invited? These things don't just happen every day!"

Laughter filled the van, along with a fair share of sniffles from Kelsey. Mr. Bones didn't know where they were going exactly, but he was happy to be here. How fast things can change! For the first time since before he saw Buck wade out into the sea, Mr. Bones was happy. Kelsey not only missed him and wanted him back, but she actually found him.

He would hold on to this moment and these feelings as long as he had them. He didn't dare hope that things couldn't change, but he was going to embrace every good feeling that came his way while they were readily available.

Enjoy the ride.

Chapter Thirty-Four

After driving a couple hours, Coco pulled the van into a campsite fifteen minutes or so off the highway. It was too dark to see much, but the group began setting up in the near pitch darkness with practiced efficiency. Tents started going up. A propane stove heated water for dinner noodles and hot beverages for those addicted to tea or coffee, even before shut-eye. Sleeping systems and night clothes appeared on the group of five. Then chairs came out around a fire pit. They all gathered around the warmth despite the warm evening, eating together, talking together, and looking for stars with ruined night vision. There was even a foldable camping chair for Mr. Bones.

"So you never named him anything different back when you had him, right?" Ariana asked Kelsey.

"I did," she responded. "I called him Amicus. Whenever I felt alone, I talked to him, which was all the time a couple of years ago. I'll probably keep calling him Amicus. I see no reason to change it or use the name he got famous with. Famous from that truck-driving jerk that stole him from me two and a half years ago."

"You might as well let it go," Travis said. "Cursing the dead won't do you any good."

"Are you superstitious?" Krumlov asked.

Travis looked at the large, darkened silhouette across the fire from him. "Not particularly, but I do recognize the pointlessness of it. The man's dead. I was just recommending let bygones be bygones."

Ariana chimed in. "Holding onto the hate isn't healthy, Kelsey. You know that. Isn't that half of the festival culture? Trying to spread the love and let go of the drama?"

Kelsey poked at her noodle soup, sitting next to Mr. Bones. "Sure. It is all of that. But I don't think any of you really understand. We found him, remember? And we *know* it is an actual skeleton. Nobody else knows that. Buck didn't know that when he took him from my yard after an ignorant request from my mother. He just—stole him. My mom didn't even care enough to help me get him back after she admitted she had no right to give him away in the first place. She let her distaste for my attachment to Amicus ruin her judgement. I don't know which was worse. Her judgement or her taste in men.

"It was messed up," Kelsey continued. "It was messed up and drowned or not. I'm going to struggle to forgive him."

The fireside grew quiet as the youths processed Kelsey's words. After several soupy slurps, Krumlov broke the silence.

"In my country," Krumlov said, "we have some beliefs about this. This—attitude—that has possessed you, Kelsey."

Krumlov's rumble demanded attention. Everyone waited for his meandering words to find them.

"We appreciate silence when nothing needs to be spoken. Sometimes saying nothing heals the most hearts. *Mluviti stříbro, mlčeti zlato,*" he said. Their faces told him the world. They didn't know what it meant, but the poetry cut through their ignorance. "Speaking is silver, silence is gold."

Kelsey smiled. "That's beautiful, Krumlov. Wise words from a culture older than ours. One more reason you're such an important part of our tribe. Well, that and you're particularly useful for scaring people when we need it." That brought laughs around the firepit. Coco, sitting next to Krumlov, addressed him.

"Can you tell us another one?"

He looked at her, his bushy dark eyebrows furrowed, making him look like someone from the Addam's Family in the firelight. "Another one?"

"She means another proverb, Krumlov," Travis said.

The caterpillar eyebrows rose into twin arches. "Oh—right." He looked at Coco and said, "Of course." Then a smile split his face that was big enough to reach from Coco's chin to the crown of her head. "A similar proverb also applies well to this talk of hate, and anger. It says—*zlost je špatný rádce*. This means anger is a bad advisor."

Krumlov looked over at Kelsey. "When you're angry about something, sometimes it is best not to listen to it. Things you say when you're angry, sometimes you regret and will want to take back later."

Zlost je špatný rádce. Mr. Bones tried to repeat the words to the best of his ability in his mind's voice. *Anger is a bad advisor.* He would ponder this when he wasn't so focused on listening.

The fire *popped*, making Coco and Travis jump. Silence rang around them, louder than most of their thoughts.

"Krumlov," Ariana said. His big eyes looked her way. "Where are you from again?" Chuckles rippled through the budding adults. "Hey, sorry," Ariana defended. "I forget! I always forget. It's embarrassing every time, but one of these days, I'm going to remember."

"It is fine," Krumlov rumbled. "I am from Czech Republic."

"Right!" Ariana said. "Czech. I remember it's poor form to ask if you're Russian, but couldn't remember which country."

"Yes. Definitely *not* Russian," Krumlov said with a laugh.

The American youths around the fire didn't get his joke, but they let it go without question. Mr. Bones had a feeling he knew, alas he couldn't comment about it either.

As the fire dwindled to embers, camp chairs started disappearing into the back of the van. Goodnights were exchanged as party members departed to sleeping pads. The last remaining fireside were Kelsey and Mr. Bones. She let the night hold the quiet for a long time, just watching the fire. Kelsey had another cup of hot tea, indifferent to the late hour. Blowing on it, she welcomed the heat into her hands. Finally, she looked over at Mr. Bones.

"The others think I'm insane for drinking hot tea in Florida," she said. "I guess that makes me a true desert dweller. I never seem to get too warm. Even in this climate."

I can't believe you found me, he said to himself, knowing she would never hear it. But he mused it anyway. *I thought I would never see you again.*

"I thought I would never see you again," she echoed, although she didn't realize he was thinking the same thing. "When Buck stole you, I went to a really dark place. I didn't speak to my mother for nearly a year. I was so angry with her. I was angry she wouldn't tell him to give you back. You aren't a toy—some stupid thing to be stolen or sold. You were a person. I don't know who you were, and that doesn't matter to me. You were *my* Amicus."

Kelsey turned in her seat to face him. "What *does* matter to me is that I found you. I made your bones more pliable and—moveable. I added the hardware to make you what you are. He had no right to take you." She shifted back towards the fire, leaning onto her knees while holding her mug. "Plenty of people that know about you think I'm ridiculous. But I don't care. Let them think I'm ridiculous. They have plenty of stupid things they think are totally normal."

Kelsey shoveled dirt around with her boot as she thought. "I've never been normal. I don't know what it feels like or what it looks like. I also don't *want* to be normal, whatever that means. If my best friend is a dead body that I found out in the desert and obsessed about for two years until I stole it back, then fine. I don't care if people don't get it. I don't get them either. With their boyfriends and their cars. Their pom-poms and perfectly fake families. And before you think about it, I'm not jealous of them. I don't want what they have."

Her eyes came up, glistening as she looked into the fire. "I want space enough to be me. Weirdly, confusing, make-no-sense me." She looked over at Mr. Bones—at Amicus—his permanent ghastly grin glowing orange from the fire. "I think that's what you represent for me. It's why I stalked Buck and followed all his social media. When I got old enough, I took all the money I saved and bought this van with some friends. It's ours. Nobody else's. I paid the biggest portion, and they all knew I was going to go looking for you someday. It was part of the deal we made together."

Mr. Bones remained in shock. He couldn't believe how much this person cared for him, and he couldn't even tell her how much it meant to him. How hard his afterlife had been. The crazy ups and downs of being dead. What a weird thing to think. The pros and cons of death. Who knew that would exist?

"It's incredible to me how cruel the world can be to someone who has never asked for anything. I was born into a 'meh' family in a crappy town out in the desert. My mother isn't terrible, but she's no pageant winner either. My absent father is likely better off away than in my life. I never did date. I don't even know if I like people like that. Travis and Ariana have been happy together for most of the time you've been gone. It's cool. Doesn't bother me. I'm glad Trav stopped hitting on me, to be honest with you. It has improved our friendship."

Kelsey looked up at the stars she could see peeking out through the boughs of trees. "I really don't know why I'm telling you all of this. I had a therapist for a while that was pretty concerned about how much I used to talk to you. Also concerned that I *missed* talking to you. I think I like it because you never tell me what to do. I can feel chill around you and no pressure at all." She looked at him. "Is that so difficult for people to understand? Maybe I just have an extreme aversion to being told what to do. In a world that constantly tells me how to feel and what to do with myself, is that *so* hard to comprehend?"

Standing, Kelsey tossed the rest of her tea into the fire. Steam hissed off the burning timber. Walking away and returning with a bucket of water that was already prepared, she doused what remained of the fire. After stirring the hot coals with a stick, she said, "I'm going to bed. Just like old times, right?" She laughed in spite of herself. Stepping closer to him, Kelsey leaned down level with his skull.

"Maybe I am insane, but that's okay. Let's be insane together. Team effort. Goodnight, Amicus. See you in the morning. It's really nice having you back." Turning, she stalked out of sight.

Just like old times, he mused. Mr. Bones thought about how it would feel to abandon what it meant to be 'Mr. Bones'. Kelsey was back. Maybe it was time to begin remembering what it was like to be Amicus instead. He decided he would think about that while practicing meditation tonight. Except this time, he would meditate on a good feeling instead of the feelings of numbness he grew so accustomed to since Buck died. What was it the Czech said?

Mluviti stříbro, mlčeti zlato. Speaking is silver, silence is gold.

It was a natural new mantra to a man who could no longer speak. Mr. Bones felt it went very well with his other mantra. He repeated them both. He imagined their resonance bringing him closer to his goal: peace.

Speaking is silver, silence is gold. Enjoy the ride.

Chapter Thirty-Five

When Amicus saw Kelsey and the gang's van in the morning light, realization swept over him. This wasn't *just* some van. It looked like they paid someone real money to outfit it for travel. Racks on the roof enabled luggage and water to be stored. Electric coolers and spare batteries took up space behind the double doors in the rear. The chassis had been lifted to provide extra clearance to negotiate modest off-road obstacles.

This van was their freedom. Freedom, home, and lifestyle welded together on wheels. It's as much a way of life as it is a symbol. This overlanding vehicle is their spirit of rebellion. Amicus thought it a thing of beauty.

After swiftly packing up camp, the crew made for the oversized rust-colored van. Coco hopped into the driver's seat and Krumlov carried Amicus. Kelsey climbed up a ladder to access the roof racks. Upon arriving at the top, she stood. "Okay, Krumlov," she said, "pass him up to me."

Krumlov extended Amicus as high as he could, which was more than high enough for Kelsey to grab hold of him. Carefully, she hauled him up to her. Carrying him princess style, she picked her path amongst luggage and containers towards the front of the van. When she set him down, it took him a moment to recognize what she designed.

Modified and bolted to the racks of the van was a wicker chair with a special seatbelt made like a pilot's harness to secure his bony frame to the seat. After setting him down, Kelsey buckled him up. "I sort of borrowed the idea from Buck, except I never liked that he put you on the front, like a dead bird stuck in the grill of his semi."

I never liked it much, either.

"So, I figured this would be a considerable upgrade," she told him. "That way you still get to see the world, but from a better vantage point! By the way, I hope you aren't too attached to the Instagram thing. I don't intend to continue doing that. Not what Buck started, and not something new. Your days of social media fame are over, Amicus. Besides, I don't want those rappers in Miami coming to look for you! Best to ride on the down-low. You know what I'm saying?"

What he thought next rattled through his existence, both living and deceased.

I think I'm comfortable not being famous anymore. No more social media. No more television. I just want to adventure with you and your friends.

She kept staring at him, almost like she was listening. He wished she could hear him. That was a puzzle he had yet to figure out. If it was possible, it remained elusive to him.

"This will be fun. I promise," Kelsey said. "You are joining us on our way to the festival of a lifetime. It's back in Nevada, but you were worth the road trip. We like the travel anyways. It's a beautiful country we have here. Be a shame not to drive across it at least once in your life. That was something Buck had right. RIP."

With that, she walked back to the rear of the van and climbed down. As she climbed in the van, Coco started the engine. He could see the campsite very well from atop their rebel spirit. His view was simple, but pretty. Broad, leafy trees were scattered across grassy ground, with a smattering of campsites and firepits mixed in. The only building he could see was the plumbing facilities.

Just like that, Amicus was back on the open road. Except this time, he was Amicus again. Kelsey had spoken true. The view from atop the van was a vast improvement from the grill of Buck's truck. Driving through the south at the end of spring was a beautiful and green experience. He thought of what Kelsey had said about their current destination. Why on earth would that girl want to leave all of this for the desert?

The road welcomed him with the sound of wind blasting against his bones while the world around him zipped by. This was a different experience than his time with Buck. This time, he was not only in a more comfortable position, but surrounded by people he loved.

His mind snagged on that realization for a moment. Surrounded by people he loved. Kelsey was obvious, but he and she were old friends at this point. She clearly loved him, too. That isn't what he'd snagged on. *People* he loved. Kelsey's friends. He pondered this for a long time. If he had anything in this world, it was time.

Amicus watched forests turn into marshlands approaching the Georgia state line and felt like a giddy child when the van crossed it. Now they drove across Georgia. The rolling hills of southern Georgia morphed into the cityscape of Atlanta. He had been to Atlanta before as Mr. Bones, and the people remembered it.

Honking erupted at the spectacle of a skeleton strapped to a chair stuck in busy inner-city traffic. He saw Mr. Boneses on the grills, tailgates, and roofs of other vehicles. Buck's legacy playing out in real time. They would have no idea that he was, in fact, the original Mr. Bones, just like they didn't know he was actually a long deceased person instead of plastic. It made him happy to see remnants of what Buck built. Business seemed to be going strong, even in the event of his death. Amicus figured it probably boosted numbers when Buck died. Such is the nature of life. You thirst for it when you realize it is fickle. Fragile. Buck's death prompted anyone who had thought of buying their own Mr. Bones, but hadn't, to do it. Go out and buy one, and strap it to your car. Participate. Live a little. Have some fun. Have even more fun, because one day you will die.

Soak up all the fun and good times that you can. Enjoy your ride.

Surrounded by people he loves, Amicus looked out over the parking lot that is the I-85 North that carries people through Atlanta. He watched the support for him and Buck's travels openly displayed on dozens of vehicles on this one stretch of highway. Buck had seen him. Saw him as a companion and—sure—as merchandise. But Buck had a dream and Amicus was witnessing its miracle first hand passing through Atlanta.

Remy and BJ had seen him as well. Recognized him. Despite their complicated intentions, they didn't mistreat him or abuse him. Without meaning to, they put him back in Kelsey's hands. He loved them for that. Looking around from his vantage point in Atlanta, he felt he loved all of these Buck supporters as well. They were just having fun. Honking like crazy at each other on the highway for fun. Each of them taking part in Buck's vision and enthusiasm for something as ridiculous as attaching a skeleton to your car for Halloween, then taking it much farther than that.

These meandering thoughts, like a slow-moving river gaining volume and momentum on its journey to the sea, were compounding as he approached a higher understanding of the world around him. He thought back to Kelsey's friends that he said he loved without thinking about it. Why would he say that? Was it simply because it was true? Could he love people he had only just met?

Honks and hanging-out-the-window yells sent them off as they broke free from the traffic. Coco participated in the honks as well. Their van was no exception in the culture of #mrbones. They were excited to have finally retrieved Kelsey's very odd friend.

He loved them because Kelsey loved them. He loved them because they seemed like great people and there was no reason *not* to love them.

What on earth was happening to him?

Chapter Thirty-Six

They camped just outside of Chattanooga, Tennessee, in a stunning grotto amidst bright beige rock spires and a curving whitewater stream. The spirit of Chattanooga echoed the sentiments of Atlanta, and they participated in customary #mrbones honks wherever they went, be it the grocery store parking lot or visiting the famous aquarium in the buzzing downtown.

Their route crossed into Kentucky, and then Illinois. Arriving in St. Louis, they received the treatment he had begun looking forward to. Another city full of honks, #mrbones swag plastered all over vehicles, and smiling faces wherever they went. That's what the brand had come to mean for Amicus. It represented happy people. Happy people just taking in a bit of fun. He had unwillingly taken center stage and became a cultural icon. An amazing feat for a dead man.

But isn't that how things worked in the world of the living more often than not? Famous after you die? Reverend Raymond Carter happened to be famous in life, now infamous and defamed, of course. Mr. Bones was famous in the afterlife as well. It made him wonder how many other souls see their legacy bloom after their physical body expires. Was this a normal phenomenon? Do others experience similar afterlives in different ways than he has? He surmised that he will never know, and never knowing is okay.

What's the fun in knowing all the secrets to life and then, thus, of death? He had spent most of his life dedicated to the search for answers and taking advantage of people who looked up to him. Guiding people, taking their money in some cases and their dignity and self-respect in others, towards what? Towards a perception of salvation? Why live your life half-way in the grave? Isn't that what he had recommended people do? To waste their lives worrying about the afterlife instead of treating each breath like the fickle things they were?

In his experience as a large plankton in the afterlife thus far, he decided if the path of Christianity is the life someone wants to lead—if it brings them happiness—then so be it. There's nothing wrong with that course of action, just don't hurt people along the way. *That* is what made his path wrong. And if his guidance was any sort of real—if God was any form of real—his current state could very well be the repercussions of that path. It was still possible whether or not he believed in God anymore.

Did it matter? Cruising atop an overlanding van across the state of Missouri as an undead Halloween prop, it didn't seem to change his afterlife in the slightest. If God intended this for him, so be it. If God wasn't real, well, so be it. His position didn't seem to change in regards to those things. Here he was, and this was the afterlife he was experiencing. He couldn't change it if he wanted to. He had, in fact, long given up trying to change it. Raymond Carter—Mr. Bones—Amicus—was just trying to enjoy the ride.

The drive continued. Amicus saw more cows and corn fields than he had ever seen in his life or afterlife. Buck and he didn't pass through this section of the mid-west. They camped on a blooming prairie outside of Kansas City. He watched the sunset over wildflowers as far as he could see, and then he watched the sunrise to the cacophonous hum of millions of insects after an all-night meditation. Learning to quiet his mind and count his gratitudes during his meditations was getting easier. Meditations were no longer haunting or numb for him, as they once were. Although born out of desperation for the absence of nothingness, of loss, they became pillars of sanity.

Within those hours of solitude, he searched for peace while accepting what he could not change. He thanked whatever entities in the wide universe that could hear his thanks. He did his best to radiate positivity in the happenstance his energy mattered elsewhere. If it didn't matter elsewhere, so be it. He would do it anyway. There was no measure or scales anymore. Amicus did it because he wanted to, and it made him feel good.

Camp was alive as the five packed up for the daily trip across state lines. Travis and Ariana assembled breakfast on a little Foreman grill. Krumlov recited poetry in Czech while Coco and Kelsey went over the route for the day. Amicus sat in his camp chair and soaked it all in. Basking in the simple joy of being surrounded by those he loved. They made his soul smile.

Nebraska and Wyoming flew by. Suddenly, they were in Utah. He didn't know where the time went. Salt Lake City greeted them as the other large cities had. Despite it being dark when they arrived, the crew pushed on. Kelsey and the gang were beyond anxious to get to their festival in Nevada, so they continued driving well into the night. Amicus saw stars like he hadn't seen in what seemed like ages. It was only months, but felt like a lifetime. Stars reminded him of the dark times after the body farm sitting alone in a heap next to the old Ford. A dark time followed by the conflagration at the hands of Kelsey, Travis, and Ariana. A necessary darkness that brought him to the light. How strange reflections like these can be.

They set up camp in the darkness amongst the Ruby Mountains off of a highway known as the Loneliest Road. Amicus thought it was a silly name. He was anything but lonely.

Chapter Thirty-Seven

Daily conversations with Kelsey at camp quickly became Amicus' favorite time of day. She told him everything he'd missed since he got stolen. How she planned to go to the University of California, Santa Cruz in the fall to study Marine Biology. This was her and her friends' jaunt together during summer, although she wanted to keep traveling in the van when she had time from school. She wasn't sure where she wanted to settle down or if she even wanted to, but Kelsey intended to take Amicus with her. He would see firsthand how her life developed as a young adult.

He sat in his chair on top of the van, enjoying his view, when the Loneliest Road came to an end. There was no sign indicating that they crossed into the Black Rock Desert, but the geography radically changed. Instead of salt flats and hard, crusty desert, it turned into chalky, fine, white dust. As the heavy treaded tires sought traction through the dust, plumes of what looked like white smoke splashed as the van plowed through. Amicus was surprised to see how many people turned up for this music event in the middle of nowhere.

Other camps had already set up real estate all over the place. Some of the vehicles were metal works of art, breathing fire, or lighting up like techno dragons. One had a working DJ booth on a platform on the roof. Music pulsed throughout every camp they drove by. Amicus went to dozens of festivals with Buck, but he had never seen anything like this.

After navigating the thumping music and hundreds of costumed guests on foot, on bicycles, on motorized fat-tired scooters and skateboards, the van stopped at a reasonably sized plot. Kelsey, Krumlov, Coco, Travis, and Ariana dismounted and excitedly began unpacking the van in a hurry. Anxious, like if they didn't have camp set up lickety-split, then they would miss the entire event.

Amicus was unloaded last, but that didn't bother him. He was still part of the journey, and that was all that mattered. Kelsey set him up in the shade next to the van, facing out underneath an easy-up. The crew set up gear he had no idea they carried with them. A water station. A hand washing station. They had an electric cooler filled to the brim with food. He knew they were eating, but never registered how much they had with them. A big amplifier appeared, and Krumlov and Coco set the camp ablaze with bass thumping music. Kelsey ran up to him, panting from the heat and exertion of running around. "Ready for your surprise?"

Amicus was ready for anything. If any blood was left in his body, it would be swimming with adrenaline and pumping through him like mad. Calling out to the group, Kelsey and the crew vanished into the van and changed into steampunk themed costumes. Part of Kelsey's costume had a seat and a harness she could attach to the back.

No way.

"Krumlov!" Kelsey yelled over the music. "Can you help me get him in?"

"Of course," the gentle giant said, and he scooped Amicus up from his cozy camp chair. Undoing the harness, Krumlov set Amicus' boney butt in the harness and fastened it around his spine and over his clavicles. The straps fed into buckles on Kelsey's shoulders. Dangling bungees went around his legs to keep them up and off the dust, cross-legged. He was beyond shocked at how the thing worked and how snug his body was held in it. Kelsey turned and gave Krumlov a hug.

"Perfect!" she yelled. She turned her head to talk over her shoulder. "You ready to party, buddy?"

Ready or not, I'm just going with the flow!

The group grabbed leather holstered canteens and insulated water bottles and took off together across the dust. They arrived at a camp done up to look like a medieval fort. Wooden barricades with spiked tops decorated their plot. The DJ played from a scaffold with a mock gallows above her. Her pink hair, gelled into big spikes that nearly touched the noose hanging down, clashed with the chain mail armor she wore. In front of the gallows were dozens of dancing festival goers. Kelsey and her crew got right into the fray, bouncing and dancing together, along with everyone else.

After the team got their fill, they bopped over to a different camp. This one mushroom-themed. Psychedelic lighting and eerie glass mushrooms covered every horizontal or vertical space. The music was slower, and electronic. At this camp, a group of two guys and a gal made friends with the crew, and they travelled to the next party plot together.

As they partied along and the multiple camps became a blur, a long-haired boy dressed like a plague doctor had joined them and took an obvious interest in Kelsey. They'd been talking and dancing together throughout the afternoon. His intentions were clear when he tried to kiss her at sunset while they were at a toxic waste-themed, yellow and green campsite party. Kelsey let him kiss her, and Amicus felt a little weird being a part of such an intimate moment. He did his best to be happy for her. She was a young woman out having fun.

And again, he had no choices besides acceptance, anyway. Might as well embrace the moment with his friend and caregiver.

Long after sunset, they made their way back to the van, and their new friends joined them. Instead of the heart-smashing, brain-pounding music that was the norm at most of the parties they attended, the group started a playlist with many hits that Amicus recognized. Everything from Pearl Jam to Phil Collins, Incubus to Ed Sheeran, The Pixies to the Weeknd. It was a good mix, and the group mingled and talked for what felt like hours.

The party disbanded and people began peeling off at their own pace. Tents went up, and conversations lulled into goodnights. Now, it was just Kelsey and the long-haired plague doctor. Cloud cover shifted and a bright waxing moon illuminated the dusty white desert. Kelsey and the boy went for a moonlit stroll together, talking and laughing, inside jokes fast developing. Amicus remained in his camp chair. He was not invited on the moonlit stroll.

He really didn't mind being alone anymore. He let this time alone speak to him. Meditation hadn't only taught him how to tune the world out, but also how to listen to it. How to participate in the universe from his narrow slice of it. To approach balance within himself regardless of the external. That's when he saw it.

Out in the far away darkness, a storm brewed. Lightning arced between clouds, illuminating them in the sky before striking downwards. Amicus waited for the sound of thunder, but it never came. That was curious.

The airborne electric charges continued and grew closer. They seemed to be coming directly towards the camp. Directly towards *him*. Something felt—amiss. Like a disturbance in the air around him. Was he tingling? Was he actually feeling something, or was it just in his mind?

Maybe the electricity was interacting with him somehow. Had he been near lightning of any kind since dying?

Another strike, only a couple of hundred feet away. Still not a sound. Lightning without thunder.

Amicus started getting concerned. Was the van safe? What about the crew? He thought of the tents scattered around their camp. Kelsey was out there somewhere. She hadn't come running back. Nobody had left any of the nearby tents. It was like nobody else could see it.

A thought hit him as another arc shot between clouds. Clouds that were eerily closing in on him. The bolt passed between them several times, coloring them deep purple and azure in the darkness before lashing out at the ground nearby. Very nearby.

The strike could have been only fifty feet away. Again, without a sound.

What if peace is what he was supposed to find? Had he grown too content? Was this a storm for him?

Was it coming for him?

Tingling within his bones grew with intensity. The storm was upon him. No one else at camp had acknowledged it. He was alone in his anxiety. Years before, early in his afterlife, he remembered thinking of the story about Owl Creek bridge. The delusion of escape before the rope snapped taut, ending the man's life. He remembered wondering if he was waiting for his rope to catch.

Electric light struck again, closer. Again, without the rumble of thunder.

Amicus wondered if this limbo was over. Was everything about to change yet again? But what if this time, what if the *new* end was coming? It seemed to happen that way thus far. The moment something seemed constant, especially good, it would be yanked from under him. Was it happening again?

Could this be the end? Could it be God coming for him? Is judgement finally ready to receive his soul? Did he even believe in God anymore?

Amicus turned away from his anxiety and sunk within himself. What did he believe? If this was what he had been waiting for, did it matter to him what came next? He no longer thought it mattered if God was calling him or if it was something else. Reflecting on every moment he'd had after death, he realized that he appreciated the time to learn more from existence. More *about* existence. The next step didn't matter as much as what he had learned. How he felt.

How he learned to love. How he had found peace while resting amidst chaos.

If that revelation wasn't enough to pass redemption, it didn't matter. Once one adopts tranquility, it is theirs to wield. Regardless of what entity, if any, holds him in judgement, he would respond the same. There would be no repenting. This was the journey—both living and dead—that he needed to find his way. Anything different would have resulted in a different resolution. When all is stripped away, you don't need rules to embrace peace. That's found within.

If anything, he believed he needed chaos for peace to find its way to him. The best thing God could have done for him was to abandon him. Alone in a wilderness of uncertainty, he found himself. He found the propensity to live in the moment and love without rules. Once learned, peace cannot be stolen.

This could be the end. If the time was upon him, he welcomed it with open arms and an open mind. If the next strike of lightning arced, and nothing happened, he accepted that. He would continue to enjoy what was in front of him. Become the present, not the past or the future.

Maybe the next bolt was meant for him—if his rope was finally about to snap—that was okay, too. Reverend Raymond Carter, turned Mr. Bones, turned Amicus—was at peace.

The sensation in his bones unfolded. Some of the first feelings since he died ignited within him, engulfing him. Soundless electricity crackled and sparked between clouds, casting an eerie light onto the camp below.

Moments are fickle. Love is worth it. Truth is forever. Enjoy the ride.

Thank you for reading *Afterlife: Experiences May Vary*
Continue on to read an excerpt from Jet Garner's debut psychological
thriller:
Death in the Afternoon

Visit **www.jetgarnerbooks.com** to join the newsletter or follow him
on social media to keep updated on his newest releases.
Instagram: **@jetgarnerbooks**
Facebook: **Jet Garner Books**
This QR Code will take you directly to his website.

Death in the Afternoon: Prologue

Nevada City, California. Wednesday, August 11, 2021

She didn't want to see him twice in one week, but he had insisted that this could be the last time, if that was what she wished. And that is definitely what she wished.

"If this is truly the last time," she had said to him when he stopped by the office in Sacramento where she worked during the day, "then okay. One last time, but no more."

Smiling, the same handsome smile that enthralled her two months before, he had agreed. "Whatever you need. If it's the last time, so be it. I mean, if you don't want the benefits anymore... Whatever you need." She had let that last statement drop without a response. It wasn't about what he was giving her. It was about how she felt every day that she lied to her husband, but he didn't need to know that.

They planned to meet at a trailhead near Nevada City, where they had met before. The trail led towards a place called Hirschman's Pond. It was a lovely hike in late August. It would be warm enough that she could wear a sundress, but cool enough that they wouldn't need to worry about overheating.

It also seemed appropriate attire and weather for what they planned to do while on the trail.

She wore a cream-colored sundress with prints of fall leaves scattered across the fabric. It was one of her favorites, and it matched perfectly with a pair of brown boots she liked to wear on short hikes.

Arriving at the trailhead parking lot early, she sat in her maroon CR-V, wondering how she was going to explain all of this to her husband. It was a relief to know that this afternoon would be the last time she had to do what she intended to do. The guilt was consuming her soul. It weighed on her like a slab of granite, smothering her. Like it could anchor her if given the chance.

Laying awake at night and staring at the ceiling while judging herself for her actions over the summer was more painful than she could bear. It was not fair to her, but it was especially not fair to her husband.

Thinking about it that way, she wasn't even being fair to the man she was meeting today, was she? No one was winning in this situation. Okay, maybe he won the most out of the three parties involved, but that doesn't matter. What matters is today would be the last time. After today, things were going to change.

She would wake up tomorrow morning and somehow broach the subject with her husband. After whatever that looked like, she would beg for his forgiveness and hope understanding would follow. Assuming he could understand. God, she hoped so. All of this was supposed to be for the better... it was supposed to help. It had simply spun out of control.

Seeing her date pull into the trailhead parking lot, she pushed all of that out of her mind for now. Being present was more important than worrying about how to fix this situation. First, she needed this arrangement to be put to rest. Checking her hair and makeup in the overhead mirror, she stepped out of her CR-V and shut the door.

"Hey," he said, walking up to her.

"Hey," she replied.

They shared a quick hug that had affection but lacked romance.

"You look good," he said.

"Thanks. You too."

He was wearing what he usually wore when she saw him. Typical blue jeans and a clean white T-shirt. It was a good look on his attractive frame.

That wasn't the issue at all.

"Well um—you wanna get going?" she said, brushing a lock of auburn hair over her ear.

"Sure, sure. Lemme just grab my pack. It has my water in it and such. You not taking any water?"

"I don't really want to be out that long. Please don't hold it against me. I'm sure you understand."

His smile faltered, but he rekindled it. "I understand. I get it. I'll be quick."

Turning, he jogged over to his truck to get the backpack. She walked across the lot to wait for him at the trailhead. She checked her phone for the time before turning it off as he came jogging back to her. It was a quarter to four in the afternoon. Killing the phone was a habit, so someone couldn't interrupt them.

"Alright, all set. Shall we?" he said.

"Sure. I'll take the lead. You remember this place from last time, yeah?"

"Yup," he said with a hungry grin. "I sure do."

Offering a half smile before turning, she said nothing in return as she stepped off on the trail.

After twenty minutes of hiking, they reached a part of the trail that opened up into a pretty clearing before arriving at the pond. It was a pleasant area to stop and relax before getting too close to the pond ahead. The marsh areas surrounding the water could harbor mosquitos even in the dry summer months, not to mention the ground itself would be boggy further in.

Where they stopped had firm woodland ground cover within the woods before the marsh. Only a few steps off the trail there was a moss covered sequoia tree that stood out from its neighbors. This wasn't a heavily trafficked trail regardless, but due to the nature of their meeting, the extra privacy provided by the trunk of the great tree was welcomed.

Leading him off the trail as she had before, she carefully stepped around the roots to put herself on the far side of the tree. In this spot, they would be out of view from the trail in the happenstance that someone walked by.

Following her around the base of the tree, his breathing was growing heavier with anticipation of what they were about to do. As she disappeared around the back side of the trunk, he took a quick look around to ensure that they were alone. Satisfied, he continued around the tree.

Her legs apart, she leaned forward with her hands against the trunk.

Stepping behind her, he removed his backpack and set it on the mossy ground. Moving his hands up her thighs and over her rump, he raised the hem of her sundress to reveal her naked sex. She had removed her panties while in the parking lot until after their deed. There was no sense in wearing them beforehand.

"This is the last time, okay? Promise me that after today, our arrangement is over. Deal?"

With a toothy grin on his face, he moved one of his hands to unzip his pants before cupping her sex with the other.

"Absolutely. Last time." His breathing had grown thick and husky.

Without further notice, he was pushing himself inside her.

She gasped at the sudden intrusion, closing her eyes. After his hands found their way around her hips, he plowed into her without remorse. Squeezing her eyes shut, she tried her best to enjoy it. Her mind raced with what she could put in her head to make all of this melt away. To warp it into something positive that she wanted to feel.

Nothing appeared in her mind except for her husband.

The slapping flump, flump, flump sound of him against her was making her regret seeing him a second time this week. What was she doing? What had she become?

As abruptly as he had begun, he stopped. Panting from exertion, he gripped her hair and moaned a last great moan.

Her face turned towards the sky. She swallowed her shame as a tear rolled down her cheek.

It will all be worth it. You have to believe that. It will all be worth it. Stay strong.

"Alright," she said. He was still inside her and holding her fast by the hair. It was difficult to speak. "I did as you asked," she said, panting between words. "Last time, right?"

Relief washed over her as his grip loosened on her hair. She took a deep breath and let her head fall forward, relaxing her neck.

"Right," he said, and then slammed the knife into her lower spine.

Her legs suddenly limp, she crumpled to the ground. She was trying and failing to find purchase with her hands on the bark of the moss covered tree.

After trying to gasp, she couldn't seem to draw a breath. Her chest felt tight and constricted. Clawing at the leaves and dirt around the moss covered roots, she desperately tried crawling away.

She heard laughter behind her.

"Hey, you needed it to be our last time, right?"

Although she couldn't see him, she could hear the grin on his sinister face.

Dragging her body with her arms, she made it back to the trail. She raised her head, hoping to see someone, a runner perhaps, making their way up the secluded trail to call for help.

None came.

"Please," she managed through gasps, "please, you don't have to do this."

Heavy foot falls made their way towards her as she crawled. Boots appeared on both sides of her. He reached and grabbed a handful of her hair.

"Oh, yes, I do. This has needed to happen for a very long time."

After pulling his pants down around his knees with his other hand, he slung her sundress above her bare buttocks before sitting on her paralyzed legs.

She heard him grunt with effort behind her, although she felt nothing. The world had suddenly turned gray in her vision as she tried to make sense of what was happening. Although breathing despite the difficulty, she couldn't move her neck from his powerful grip on her hair. Any attempt she made to move her legs had proved useless. From his grunting and the way her body rubbed back and forth against the ground, she had a clear grasp of what he must be doing. Fear was moving up the good half of her spine, wondering why she couldn't feel it.

With a loud exhale, he moaned his completion. Her eyes darted around like a bunny caught by the ears. He hadn't let go of her yet. She still couldn't move her head. Her arms pushed against the ground, helpless against his weight and strength.

"I hope you understand. It isn't anything that you did." He pushed her forehead hard against the dirt of the trail. "You just married the wrong man."

Confused and suddenly weak, she couldn't press against the earth any longer. Her arms went slack as she tried to swallow the dryness in her throat.

Tears formed in her eyes. Her husband appeared in her mind again. Shame welled up inside her, knowing that she wouldn't be able to explain this to him. She wished she could see him again. Even if just one last–

The thought was cut short when the blade plunged into the base of her skull.

COMING SOON

NEXT PSYCHOPOMP NOVEL

AVAILABLE EARLY 2025

JET GARNER

About Author

Jet Garner is an American Navy Veteran and nomadic author. An avid adventurer and world traveller, he draws from his experiences and destinations to fuel his storytelling. Born in Mississippi and raised in Jackson, Tennessee, Thailand was his last place of residence at the time of publishing this book. Currently, he is traveling throughout Southeast Asia with his wife, Crystal, while working on his next novel.

.